**BLOOD SUCKING SERIES NO. 1**

# THE FINAL FLOOR

*NORMA LINENBERGER*

PublishAmerica
Baltimore

© 2007 by Norma Linenberger.
All rights reserved. No part of this book may be reproduced, stored in a retrieval system or transmitted in any form or by any means without the prior written permission of the publishers, except by a reviewer who may quote brief passages in a review to be printed in a newspaper, magazine or journal.

Second printing

All characters in this book are fictitious, and any resemblance to real persons, living or dead, is coincidental.

PublishAmerica has allowed this work to remain exactly as the author intended, verbatim, without editorial input.

Hardcover 9781630048563
Softcover 9781630042011
PUBLISHED BY PUBLISHAMERICA, LLLP
www.publishamerica.com
Baltimore

Printed in the United States of America

## DEDICATION:

This book is dedicated to my husband Leo and family, Debbie, Cherie, Elva, Jackie, Jeff, Jimmy and Valerie. Grandchildren Milah, Morgan, Cayden and Dayton.

## SPECIAL THANKS TO:

My daughter Jackie for her help, my son, Jimmy, for the title, and my granddaughter, Milah, for her input on a small part of the book.

# Introduction

Walking home from work on a dark, cold, blustery night, is only the mild beginning of an otherwise bloody rampage through the Rockwood Apartment Complex by an unknown assailant. Mystery coupled with suspense and murder clouds the mind to the last page as the characters unfold into view.

For those of you that enjoy the imaginative thriller type murder mystery, the following forthcoming chapters are highlighted with unique and unusual circumstances surrounding the mysterious deaths of a variety of characters.

As a new author of my first book, "The Final Floor," I hope you will enjoy the cast of characters, setting and the plot incorporated into the writing of this book. It was a rewarding experience for myself and "thank you" for reading "The Final Floor."

# Chapter 1
# Chicken Soup—1995

Police patrol the streets all night long in this small, mid-western city of Rockwood, Illinois. Thus, they encountered Sue Benson walking home from work one evening. Her shoulders hunched forward, as she lowered her head to ward off a cold blast of wintry air.

"Sue! It's cold out there and beginning to snow. Are you all right? Can we give you a ride home?" Officer Green and Officer Leeds yelled as they pulled up along side of her. "No thank you, officer. I'm just about at the Rockwood apartment building and my mother is waiting for me," said Sue.

"Okay, see ya," as they sped off into the night muttering to themselves. "Go ahead and walk back to the apartment in this crappy weather! See if we care! That's your own fault," the officer yelled.

Sue is dreaming of her mother's homemade chicken soup amidst thoughts of what had transpired the morning before at the apartments. As she is walking home, her memory reflects on the incident and on the impact it would leave on the remaining tenants. She was in a turmoil as numerous questions entered her mind. Namely, who actually did kill Fern Taylor? Where was her killer at this very moment? Was he lurking in the shadows ready to claim his next victim? Was it safe to walk home alone after 11:00 at night? Maybe she should have taken a ride home with the police or at least have called Dyke's Taxi Service. It was stupid walking by herself on such a lone stretch and on a damn, bitter, cold night.

This small mid-western city of Rockwood, Illinois, leaves a lot to the imagination. Rockwood dots the landscape between Maplesville and Bixby, north of Interstate 70 and is in the western part of Illinois with the county seat in Larsen County. In this small city of Rockwood, everybody knows everybody else. You can't remain a stranger in a town of 12,479 people without being recognized once in awhile.

The town's eleven churches and the American Legion Post 1249 are the hub of social gatherings. Townspeople congregate for coffee at Barb's Café on Main Street or the Red Diamond Motel coffee shop on the edge of town on Interstate 70. The local movie theatre, The Rockwood Cinema, has been open for fifty-four years and still generates a lot of business on the weekends. If an outstanding feature is being shown, they are open extra nights. The local newspaper, The Rockwood Flyer, is still in existence. It is six pages long and the local people look forward to each day's printing, advertisements and pictures.

Rockwood College has 1,271 students enrolled and there are 342 students employed within the city and outlying communities. Many local residents patronize the college by their attendance at their sports games, plays and educational programs. There is a good relationship between Rockwood College and the city of Rockwood.

Sue finally reached the ten story apartment building on Logan Street. She is a young forty-five year old divorcee of ten years who moved in with her mother immediately after her divorce. Her finances did not allow her to compete with today's society and live on her own. She has two grown children. Albert, twenty, is a single clerk working in the Marriott Hotel in Calgary, Canada, while Jean is twenty-three, also single and works at the Mitchell Finance Company in Boston, Massachusetts. Sue's husband, George's, whereabouts is unknown. George was last seen five years ago at the bus terminal purchasing a ticket for New York City. Sue and her mother, Jane, have lived in the Rockwood apartment building for ten years. Sue is the short, stocky, matronly type with wispy, brunette hair, brown eyes and a contagious laugh. She is a college graduate, good natured and easily likeable by anyone who comes in contact with her, a reflection of her mother, Jane.

Sue's mother, Jane, is sixty-six years old. A sweet, good-natured person of humble descent, a tall, willowy, framed woman with short, gray hair, Jane has the bluest eyes of anyone. She lived her life as a housewife by trade. Jane and her husband, Bob Linton, and Sue, their only child, lived in Blueville, Illinois, before moving to Rockwood ten years ago. Sue's seventy-one year old dad worked in a luggage factory in Rockwood before succumbing to heart failure this past spring. Sue took total charge of her mother after her father passed away.

As Sue steps slowly inside, she proceeds to the fireplace to warm her hands. A few of the tenants are playing cards, while a few others are watching a Christmas program on television, since it is two weeks before Christmas. Several others are having a fireside chat, which she joins.

"I'm worried about what happened to Fern Taylor yesterday morning," Nick, one of the tenants, said. "My wife, Sarah, is more scared than I am. I'm wondering if we should buy a car instead of walking all over, but the doctor said I should walk after my heart surgery, so I'm trying to obey his instructions."

"I enjoy walking in the early morning, inhaling the fresh air, the hustle and bustle of this little city and the limbering up of my old joints. We always feel more relaxed and rejuvenated when we come back," Sarah joined in." When we are experiencing inclement weather, Nick and I go to Brooks Exercise Center downtown. After that, we stop at Barb's Café for a cup of coffee."

Nick and Sarah Jones have only resided at the apartment for two years. They are both retired, professional people, having spent a total of thirty-five years working at the Office of Administration at Rockwood College and are both natives of the city.

Sue made the comment, "I was a little apprehensive about walking home from work this evening. I had conjured all kinds of thoughts in my mind. Periodically, I looked back over my shoulder to see if I was being followed, because at one point, I thought I heard footsteps. I was probably just imagining things. Office Leeds and Officer Green offered to give me a ride home, but I declined. Maybe, that wasn't such a good idea? What do you think?" Sue asked.

# Chapter 2
# Fern Taylor's Murder—1995

Joe Mellow, a resident of the apartments, blurted out his testimony of what he saw, "Well, I told everybody what I witnessed yesterday when Fern was murdered. I opened the door early, around 6:00 AM. to pick up the newspaper and I happened to glance toward the elevator because of a loud noise. The elevator door was closed but I saw blood seeping underneath the door and out into the hallway. All of a sudden, the elevator door partly opened and I could see that Fern's eye glasses had flown off her face and fallen onto the floor. Poor Fern, her vision was limited as it was and I'm sure that instilled even more fear in her. I saw someone beating her with their fists, over and over again, as her face turned ashen gray and her eyes began to swell and bleed. I could also hear Fern striking someone with her cane and screaming repeatedly for help, but to no avail. I started screaming and feared for my own life, as the person in the elevator yelled at her with an unusual, almost feminine voice saying, "You old fool! I hate people like you! You remind me of my own mother and I hated her! You won't leave this elevator alive!"

"I kept screaming for help, but no one arrived," Joe said. "As I continued looking toward the elevator door, I could make out a long sleeved arm similar to a woman's. In a blur, I saw the arm pull out a long knife and penetrate Fern's heart numerous times with multiple stab wounds. All of a sudden the knife stuck within Fern's heart, only to protrude out of her back. Blood, vomit and bile gushed out of Fern's mouth as her eyes were wide open suddenly and rolled back in her head. A groan escaped her lips as her eyelids closed in death and her body went limp. As she slumped to the floor, the killer dashed down the hallway and out the side entrance, heading down the street or alley as several tenants said they saw footprints on the driven snow."

Mr. Phillips and his wife, May, the landlords and other tenants arrived too late on the grisly scene. Everybody was shaking, weeping and fearful of the gruesome homicide that had occurred. Joe Mellow called the police while Mr. Phillips contacted the paramedics. When they arrived, they covered Mrs. Taylor's body with a black shroud and carried her eighty-nine pound frame out on a stretcher to await the ambulance. Joe Mellow was transferred by car to the police station where he furnished them with all the information that he had witnessed.

Sue also reported to the police about seeing a woman loitering in the apartment building, when she came home the night before. Maybe, it was just a coincidence. Who knows for sure? Sue explained her version:

"I was devouring my mother's chicken soup and discussing the day's activities with her listening, as usual, making a comment now and then. About 10:00 PM the phone rang and it was one of my close friends from the office, Mary Bowles, asking me if I would spend the night at her house because she didn't feel well and didn't want to be by herself. I told her I would be right over as soon as I finished packing an overnight bag and a change of clothes for work, so I wouldn't have to come back to the apartment in the morning. Mother said she would be fine by herself and to go ahead."

For some unknown reason, the next morning, Sue felt uneasy about leaving her mother, so she went back to check up on her around 8:00 AM. She was fine, just like she said she'd be. Jane made some coffee, sausage, biscuits and gravy for breakfast, so they proceeded to eat, but didn't finish.

# CHAPTER 3
# EVACUATION—1995

"Everybody is being evacuated because of something that happened a couple of hours ago. Please refer to Dan's Diner for the duration of the search of the Rockwood Apartment building. The wind chill factor is five below zero and everyone is to bundle up and gather in the main lobby for further instructions," the loud speaker announced at 8:30 AM.

Immediately, the frightened tenants could be seen coming down the stairway clinging to each other consumed with fear and utter desperation. When Mr. Phillips, the seventy-four year old landlord of nine years, met with the sixty-five tenants, he explained the circumstances of the evacuation. Mr. Phillips is small in stature with thin, graying hair, bespectacled and walking with a limp.

"There has been a horrible murder committed in the main elevator at the Rockwood Apartment building. Please remain in Dan's Diner until the police give the 'All Clear' signal for you to return to the building," suggested Mr. Phillips to the apartment dwellers.

The alarm grips the tenants as they proceed single file to Dan's Diner across the street. The evacuees huddled together in the Diner plotting their next move, while others planned to post watches around the inside of the building. They were to report any unfavorable characters loitering around the inside or outside of the building from this day forward.

It was getting late in the morning and everybody was finished discussing the events of the homicide except to comment about Fern herself. Mrs. Taylor was an eighty-five year old widow who lived in the apartment building for five years after her husband passed away. Fern's husband, Oliver, had been a local cab driver and Fern had retired as a day cook from the college. Their three children are scattered in various states and have already been notified. She lived a quiet life, minding her own business. Every morning around 6:00 AM, Fern could be seen crossing the street to Dan's Diner from the Rockwood apartment building for her usual morning coffee and a bite to eat. But, this morning was different. Sly, creepy eyes had been watching Fern's apartment for days and then slowly slinking away, as Fern left the apartment building. Somehow, they retraced her steps and slipped into the backside of the elevator after she had come in and immediately took her life.

George Sloan was quoted as saying, "This murder might escalate into more victims! Mary and I aren't going to hang around town to be counted among the dead! I seriously think it's time to leave. Does anybody else want to come along? Speak up now, if you do!" They were considering moving to a safer location.

Everyone was stunned and exceedingly quiet. "We're debating whether we should leave, also. It's not worth living in a nice apartment day in and day out if you have to fear for your life at nightfall," said Lloyd Sharp.

As the residents aired their grievances, they sipped their hot, steamy coffee out of cheap, ceramic mugs, stomping out one cigarette after the next in nervous exasperation, not knowing what else to do. Nobody relished the idea of nightfall approaching any more, for fear of a repetition of Fern Taylor's death.

The next day at mid-morning, the Rockwood police came into Dan's Diner and gave the "All Clear" signal for the tenants to return to their apartments. Many were skeptical about going back, while others were thinking about spending more time together. Some preferred watching television or visiting by the fireside in the main lobby.

Fern Taylor's body was buried at a much later date amidst family, relatives and friends at an undisclosed location on a cloudy, cold, wintry day. Her casket was in full view as family and friends paid their last respects. An unknown woman was the last mourner to pay her respects, since she was lurking in the background. She was also the first person to leave.

One evening, as Sue was walking through the main lobby of the Rockwood apartments, she encountered the woman sitting in the lobby and reading the newspaper. She smiled at her and said, "Good evening, Ma'am." To which she replied, "Good evening, Ma'am," and Sue bolted out the door harboring an uneasy feeling about her.

# CHAPTER 4
# PINOCHLE—1995

    Her day at the Murphy Finance Company went fairly smooth for a Monday. Mondays were usually pretty hectic following a weekend, but today was different. As she closed her books and straightened up her reports, she happened to look across the street. What caught her eye was not only a man, but a woman with him peering across the street at her. As quickly as she saw them, is as quickly as they disappeared. By this time, it was already dark, so Sue grabbed her coat and briefcase and hurried along. At this point, she had only three blocks to walk with no one insight except a few cars passing her on the street. The Rockwood apartments, dark and forbidding, loomed in the foreground as she entered the door. She stepped into the lobby to warm her hands by the fireplace and chatted with a few friends before proceeding to the elevator to go to her apartment.

    Rich asked Sue to join them in a game of pinochle. Sue said she would go and ask her mother also, if she would want to join them in a game of cards. She took the elevator up to the apartment and asked her mother. Jane said, "No, because I'm going to watch a little television and retire early. Tell them, thank you for asking me. I'm sure I'll play cards with them some other time. They're all pretty good card sharks, I'm sure. Sue, you go on down and play cards with them if you want. I'll be fine."

"Mother, are you sure?" Sue asked.

"Of course I am," Jane replied. "Run along now. Besides, I'm getting a splitting headache."

Sue said, "O. K." She left the apartment for the lobby. When she got down there they were all seated around the dark, oak table in the recreation parlor. Rich was shuffling and dealing the cards with a score sheet beside him. Playing were Sue, Rich, Bob and Ella Cain and George Sloan and his wife, Mary. Before Sue sat down, she refilled everybody's coffee cup and the cookie platter.

As the card game progressed, Sue glanced toward the window and said, "Hey everybody, it's snowing and blowing outside. Who wants some more coffee?" A few raised their hands and she said, "Coming right up."

All of a sudden the front door of the apartment complex opened up ushering the "loner". He smiled and said, "Hello," and proceeded to warm his hands by the fireplace with his basket of belongings accompanying him. As soon as Rich saw this, he invited him to play pinochle and they picked teams.

"Are you playing for money?" asked the "loner". "No, pull up a chair and I'll deal you a hand," Rich replied.

"Okay, that's fair enough. What have I got to lose besides sleep and I can sleep anywhere. I've even slept in here already on that blue sofa over by the wall. When I do that I'm real close to my work across the street at Dan's Diner. I'm sorry. I guess I've never introduced myself. My name is Marcus Reil. And where am I from? I know that's what you're all thinking. I'm from Nowhere, U.S.A. I've been a drifter most of my life. No place to call home. How about you guys? I can tell you're all pretty well established here. When you're in a retirement center, you usually are not out working in the public anymore. Right?"

Rich replies, "No, none of us are working out anymore. We've all retired except for Sue Benson and a few younger couples."

While they are conversing back and forth they are still engrossed in the game with Marcus' team winning. They continued to snack on cookies and coffee, offering Marcus some, which he gratefully accepted since he hadn't eaten supper for lack of money.

They played Pinochle till about 11:00 p.m. with Marcus' team winning. They decided to go to their room. "Does anybody want to play cards tomorrow night?" Rich asked. They all said yes, including Marcus. "We will meet here at 7:00 p.m." Rich added. "Good night, everybody."

Marcus decided to sleep at the Rockwood apartments for the night on the blue sofa with an old pillow and blanket, because he had to be at work at Dan's Diner across the street at 6:00 a.m. So he switched off the television set and turned in for the evening, sleeping in his street clothes.

At 6:00 a.m. sharp, Marcus is pushing his basket across the street with all his worldly possessions inside, ready to go to work until 2:00 p.m. The customers are streaming in while Marcus is washing his first load of dishes in between sips of hot coffee, an egg and bacon off the griddle. A few men from the apartment came into the diner for breakfast and saw Marcus and yelled, "Good morning, Marcus. Did you sleep well?" To which he replied

"Yes, very well."

"Remember, our 7:00 card game in the recreation parlor tonight," the men said. "I'll be there," Marcus said and kept on washing dishes. The men finished their breakfast and went back to the apartment since there is supposed to be a blizzard moving in from the western part of the United States.

# Chapter 5
# The Rattlesnake—July, 1997

In spite of the years that have passed, everything seems to be back to normal except Fern Taylor's murder case isn't solved and her killer hasn't been brought to justice. Several tenants moved to better locations, while sixty-one continue to stay together as a group, spending more time in the lobby, going to movies, sharing meals together and walking home as a group. The apartment dwellers blend in together because it is mostly older, retired people plus a few younger couples. The apartments are well maintained and reasonably priced.

On any given day, a person can see residents coming and going in broad daylight, but not too many at night. If they go out at night, they do as a group and come back as a group. On different occasions, because of inclement weather, they've been known to share a taxi.

So, it is with Bob Cain, an eighty-six year old retired school teacher who shares an apartment with his wife, Ella, of 55 years. Bob is your typical tall, six-foot man weighing about 225 pounds. His thick, white hair has thinned out over the years and now he is left with a bald crown and a fringe. Bob is the gruff, yet a soft-spoken type. He taught in the Rockwood Grade School system for twenty four years teaching fifth and sixth grade English and math.

Ella suffered a stroke and her walking was slightly affected, so now Bob dines out with the apartment group once a week. Ella is 84 years old, a small framed woman with thinning, reddish brown hair, a curvaceous smile and pleasing personality. Ella spent her life as a housewife dedicated to her husband and six children.

"Ella, I'm going downstairs to the lobby to get our mail. I'll be right back," Bob said to Ella.

"Okay," said Ella as she smiled up at her husband.

Bob entered the elevator on the third floor using his walker. He is totally deaf in one ear and can't hear very well out of the other ear. So if someone or something approaches him in the elevator, he would never hear it.

Bob accidentally turned around and in the elevator lay an Arizona, six foot long rattlesnake with his fangs protruding, full of venom, poised to strike. "Oh! No! Help me, someone! I'm going to die! No! Get away from me," Bob screamed.

The snake's rattlers were very loud as it hissed and struck Mr. Cain in the chest and heart. Venom penetrated his bloodstream with some even falling on the elevator floor. Amidst continuous screams of pain and agony, the elevator stopped on the lobby floor. The door swung open and Mr. Cain had collapsed on the elevator floor close to death. Several people witnessed this tragedy and Rich called an ambulance while Fred notified his wife. Ella hobbled to the elevator and was beside herself with grief and fear. "Oh, no, Bob! Please, someone help him. Help him! He's dying," screamed Ella.

About this time, the ambulance came and the paramedics covered his 225-pound frame with a sheet and transported him to Rockwood Hospital where he was pronounced dead upon arrival at 8:42 p.m. Ella ordered an autopsy taken of her husband at The Brown Mortuary. The results indicated toxic snake venom in the bloodstream amongst other things.

Several men in the apartment building came to the assistance of the maintenance supervisor, bringing a mesh net to cast over the rattlesnake. It slithered and writhed on the elevator floor, ready to strike out at anybody in its presence. They captured the rattlesnake on the first try, sealed the net and carried it to their vehicle for disposal; its rattlers still going strong.

The media, police and detectives were called once again to the Rockwood apartments to the scene of the death of Mr. Cain. They scattered to the four corners in search of the assailant going door to door, questioning people and interviewing suspects who had access to a large rattlesnake in the middle of summer. Everybody's questions were, "Where did this reptile come from? How did he slither into the apartment building unnoticed? Did someone deliberately put him in the elevator? Will another snake appear?"

Detective Jones has no leads to this unusual crime as he visits the local zoo in search of a missing rattlesnake. All rattlesnakes are accounted for in their cages, twelve to be exact. He also traveled on to the neighboring cities of Millsburg and Plattsville to question the zoo keepers, but no rattlesnakes had been taken from the zoo. They came to the conclusion that someone was harboring a large rattlesnake in their home, basement or garage.

The apartment dwellers gathered at the Brown Mortuary for the final viewing of Bob Cain's body. Upon entering the private room of Bob, we see Ella and her six children sitting in the mourner's row as people file by to pay their last respects to Bob and extend their condolences to Ella and her family. Bob is clad in a dark suit, clean shaven, his hair neatly combed and a calm, serene look on his face.

Once again, the residents of the apartment building gathered at Rockwood Cemetery to mourn the passing of Bob Cain. An intense heat accompanied the residents as they struggled to keep their composure amidst crying, sniffling and saddened hearts. As they gathered around the casket for their final goodbyes, an unknown man and woman appeared back amongst the mourners. As the preacher conducted the memorial service, they peered suspiciously at everyone there and then left.

# Chapter 6
# The Bar Room Brawl—1998

As winter finally comes to an end, spring is fast approaching. With trees budding, flowers in bloom and lawns sprouting green grass, days are getting longer with people spending more time outdoors. Everything smells green. Lawns are neatly manicured while children play in the parks, couples take long walks and bicyclists tour the city and shoppers take to the malls.

By now, an unfamiliar man has been seen walking freely on the city streets of Rockwood, unrecognized, just one of the crowd. He is indeed a loner, not mingling with anyone, a drifter at heart. He can be seen on the campus of Rockwood College occasionally talking to a college student. He frequently rides the local transit bus from the college to the downtown area. No family, no transportation of his own and no job except for washing dishes at Dan's Diner once in awhile. No ties to anybody or anything. Truly, a lost soul.

He can also be seen at the local cafes and restaurants eating his meals and sleeping on a city park bench with a newspaper over his head as the days get warmer.

Tenants of the apartments reported him to the local police department and they questioned him on different occasions, but couldn't find anything to keep him in custody. They had no choice but to release him. The routine interrogation included, "Where were you on May 12, the night of the rattlesnake murder at 8:15 p.m.," the detective asked.

"I went to the theater and I have proof because the girl in the concession stand recognized me. Do you want me to give you her name?" asked Marcus.

"There's a possibility we'll need that name later on. Hold on to your information," replied the policeman.

A good alibi? The police questioned him repeatedly about Fern Taylor's murder in the elevator on December 13, 1995.

"I distinctly remember that morning because I was working at Dan's Diner washing dishes and we could look across the street at the apartment building and see the police and the crowd of people congregated outside. The media and the police came into the diner and asked us if we noticed anything unusual at the apartment that morning and we all said no. I can verify this with my boss, Dan Blythe. Do you need verification?" asked Marcus.

"We'll let you know," said the police. "It's been reported that you have been seen sleeping in the lobby of the Rockwood apartment building on different occasions. Do you not have a home? Are you a vagrant? Do you have any family in town?" remarked Detective Jones.

"I came here years ago to attend Rockwood College but I couldn't keep up with the finances so I dropped out of college and wound up homeless. So, yeah, I live on the streets. I found out it was so simple to sleep in the lobbies of apartment buildings and on park benches, especially in the spring and summer when it is warmer. I got a two-bit job washing dishes to buy my meals and do laundry. I'm completely harmless, officer. No one needs to be frightened of me because I wouldn't harm anybody. I never have and I never will," explained Marcus.

Roam the streets he does for a couple of years, but that is changing. Almost daily he frequents Joe's Bar for a drink and light conversation with the local patrons. On one such occasion, he casually strolled into the bar and started making small talk with the man next to him, Earl Mills. Earl is an unemployed sub-contractor for Berg Construction. By this time, patrons can hear Marcus screaming and slamming his fists on the bar. "Shut your damn mouth! I didn't say anything of the sort. You'd better not be calling me a liar. You don't know where I came from or where I'm going. Nobody does and I don't owe you an explanation, you nut," screamed Marcus.

"I don't care where in the hell you crawled out from, because your type is equivalent to or worse than trailer trash. Get away from me! You remind me of the devil re-incarnated," replied Earl.

"Oh! You're poking fun of me? I wouldn't poke too much fun of me if you know what's good for you!" said Marcus, as his eyes sparked with red, hot rage and his voice lowered to a growl.

"Don't be telling me what's good for me! I can round up several guys in here to beat the hell out of you and easily leave you for dead," said Earl.

The men flew off their stools, facing each other with eyes glaring and fists clenched, ready to make their next move. About this time, the bartender called the local police to report the brawl. They came immediately, guns straddling their hips and escorted Marcus, handcuffed, off to jail for one week on charges of disorderly conduct in a place of business.

After his dismissal from Rockwood jail, he could be seen at all the local places again, reading the newspaper on park benches, riding the bus, loitering in public buildings and hanging out in local restaurants. But things have changed. Upon his release, the police warned him, "Get a decent job or get out of town."

# Chapter 7
# A New Job

Shuffling Along in a Blinding Rainstorm Toward the Rockwood Apartments pushing his cart of accumulated, prized, personal possessions Marcus muttered to himself, "Oh hell, I know what the police said, get a decent job or get out of town. Where am I supposed to get a decent job in this town? I barely make enough money to buy my meals and do my laundry, much less buy a car or rent an apartment. I need a better job than washing dishes at Dan's Diner, for crying out loud."

As he entered the apartment building sopping wet, he said, "I don't have to work tomorrow, so I'll go to sleep now already. That way I'll be up bright and early to be one of the first ones in line up at the unemployment office." The tenants all looked at each other and acted as if they didn't hear his voice, as they proceeded to their apartments early after they finished singing and playing cards. Marcus lay on his favorite blue divan against the wall in the recreation parlor with a pillow and spare blanket.

Marcus quit Dan's Diner, because he was so excited about applying for a job that he could hardly contain himself, so consequently he didn't sleep much that night. He was up bright and early for breakfast at Dan's Diner across the street. After a good breakfast he headed down the street to the unemployment office and got in his application for a janitor job at the college. Many applicants were there but Marcus was first. After he filled out his application and presented it to the clerk, she explained that he would be contacted within a couple of weeks at Dan's Diner if they were interested in hiring him. He said, "Okay" and left the unemployment office, to wander aimlessly around. He continued to drift in and out of the Rockwood Apartment Building watching television, visiting with the tenants and playing cards on certain nights with the card players, including Sue and her mother Jane. After they went to their apartments, Marcus would spend the night on the blue divan against the wall and be gone before 6:00 AM in the morning to Dan's Diner across the street. On different occasions he also spent nights at the Wildflower Inn down the street, a repetition of the Rockwood Apartment Building, in regards to visiting with the tenants, card games, television, and singing anything to pass the time.

Two weeks has passed since Marcus applied for the janitor job at Rockwood College. On Monday morning as he was washing dishes at Dan's Diner he received a call from the unemployment office telling him, "You have been hired as janitor at the college and when can you report for work?" He said, "I can report for work the next day, Tuesday." The voice at the other end of the line said, "Fine, Thank you," and hung up. Marcus had his instructions to be at the job training center at Rockwood College at 7:00 AM for work. An assistant trainee accompanied Marcus through the building and briefed him on the different phases of janitorial cleaning that he would be exposed to. They inspected the janitorial closets and Marcus was shown samples of floor washing with a mop and different kinds of cleaning and waxing liquids and techniques.

As the weeks went by Marcus continued to do well at his janitor job. He takes the local transit bus to and from the college to the Rockwood Apartments and works from 7:00 AM till 3:00 PM with one hour off for lunch. He eats his breakfast and supper meals at Dan's Diner and his dinner at the college cafeteria.

About midweek he plays cards with the regular card players for entertainment in the recreation parlor. One evening as the conversation drifted towards Marcus' job, he boldly announced, "I've been working about a month now and I think I'll buy myself a cheap second hand car to get around town instead of taking the bus back and forth to work. I can make payments until it's paid for. It's cheaper buying a car than taking the bus every day. It's also getting very unhandy to wash my work uniforms every week at the laundromat. I also need some more clothes. I'm accumulating too much to push in my cart, because I noticed it's getting too heavy. Does anybody have any suggestions?

"I think I have a good idea provided you can afford it?" Rich said "Get yourself a car like you said and when you are well established with the car you might start thinking about getting yourself an apartment. After you get an apartment you should be pretty well taken care of. We'll all help you get settled in. Just say when.

Again, bright and early the next day, Marcus walked downtown to several car dealers to look at their used cars and test drive them. He finally settled on a 1985 green Ford with 100,000 miles on the odometer. The price of the car was $1,500.00, with $125.00 a month car payments.

As summer is fast approaching, on occasion, Marcus has been known to sleep in his car with his belongings, parked in front of the Rockwood Apartment building.

In the evening Marcus can be seen driving his Ford when he isn't working up and down Main Street. Once in awhile his girlfriend, Betty Jones, can be seen with him but never driving his car.

On Wednesday evening Marcus and Betty played pinochle at the Rockwood Apartments with the card players. Sue asked Marcus, "How do you like your car, Marcus?" To which he replied, "I like it real well and so does Betty. It's better than walking all over town, getting sore feet. The air conditioner doesn't work, but that's okay because we can always roll the windows down. Anyway, maybe one of these days after it's paid off I'll have the air conditioner repaired. I can't financially do everything all at one time because my finances won't allow it. One of these days I still want to get my own apartment. Betty has an apartment on Lindsay Street, but basically I still sleep in my car or in the Rockwood Apartment lobby."

Betty Jones, 41, Marcus' girlfriend, has decided to quit her low paying job at Pillar's Flower Shop and work as a janitor at Rockwood College for the same amount of money. So, yesterday morning she applied at the college for a janitor's job and she will be notified in several weeks. Time passed and she received a call yesterday telling her she could start Monday morning at 7:00 AM, the same as Marcus because he can pick her up on the way to work.

It is the middle of July and Marcus has decided to get himself an apartment because of sleeping in the hot car all night. He has been checking the "apartments for rent" in the local news paper. A furnished one bedroom apartment will suffice, but not too expensive. Marcus found an apartment immediately on Poller Street, three blocks east of Main Street. Betty lives on the west end of town in a new housing development with her parents. A group of card players from the Rockwood Apartments offered to help him get situated, buying things he needs for his apartment. Now he doesn't have to sleep in the lobby of the Rockwood Apartments anymore, nor in his hot car all night which could be dangerous.

Marcus' apartment has been uninhabited for awhile and is in dire need of a good cleaning, so his card playing friends including Sue and her mother Jane and his girlfriend Betty Jones have decided to give the apartment a complete cleaning while Marcus is at work.

When Marcus came home from work that might he was shocked when he walked into his apartment clean as a whistle. He said, "I want to thank everybody that helped clean my apartment today, because it was something I was dreading already. May God bless you for your labor and generosity. Thank you, again!"

Towards evening after everybody left Marcus ate supper and then sat down to watch a little television before retiring. All of a sudden the phone rang and it was Marcus' brother, Adam, telling Marcus that their 82 year old dad had passed away about twenty minutes ago, of a sudden heart attack. Marcus was extremely shocked as he talked to his mother and the rest of the family saying, "As soon as I hang up the phone I'll shower, pack my bags and be on my way to St. Louis. I bought myself a car and I'll see you sometime tomorrow. Bye!"

## BLOOD SUCKING SERIES NO. 1: THE FINAL FLOOR

Before he hung up his mother said, "Marcus, the funeral is pending notification of next of kin." After Marcus hung up he immediately called his janitorial supervisor for a leave of absence from his job for several days because he was driving to St. Louis for his dad's funeral. He also called Betty, his girlfriend, and his friends at the Rockwood Apartment Complex telling them, "My 82 year old dad passed away tonight and I'm leaving for St. Louis in a little while. I'll be back in a couple of days. Bye!" They all extended their sympathy and wished him a safe trip to St. Louis.

He hung up and quickly took a shower, dressed, packed his suitcase which he had just purchased and left for St. Louis at 9:00 PM. He knew he would be arriving in St. Louis in the wee hours of the morning, so he drank plenty of coffee before he left to stay awake. It was August 12$^{th}$ and it had been a blistering hot day, but it was beginning to cool down and a light mist was beginning to form on the windshield the longer he drove. He used his windshield wipers as he went down the highway to the blare of an all night St. Louis radio station. About midnight he turned into an all night diner for a cup of coffee and the current edition of the local newspaper. As he sat in a booth by himself next to a window, he noticed the soft mist had turned to light rain. He finished his coffee and newspaper and decided to move on since he was still in Illinois. He drove all night long and finally arrived in Missouri. He still had a couple of hundred miles to go to get to St. Louis, and the sky was beginning to lighten up as he pulled into another all night diner for breakfast which tasted delicious since he was starved. At this point he is on the last leg of his trip and about 200 miles East of St. Louis. He relaxed in the diner for awhile and then decided to continue on as he didn't have that much farther to go.

Finally around 9:30 AM he pulled into the driveway of his childhood home as his mother and family came out to greet him amidst hugs and kisses. A joyful reunion on such a sad occasion with his brother, Adam and sisters, Clare and Vivian.

After the family visited for an extended length of time it was almost dinner time. Marcus wasn't hungry and excused himself because he had been driving all night long and was very tired and sleepy. He went to his boyhood bedroom and dropped off to sleep.

The next day brought numerous relatives and friends to the New Found Baptist Church that Marcus can remember attending as a young boy. The casket was open with Marcus' father Dwight in full view. He was dressed in a black suit and tie, his thick gray hair neatly combed and a peaceful, calm, serene look on his face. After church services the body was transported to St. Louis Cemetery for burial which had a nice representation of people.

They had a full luncheon in the church basement for family, friends and out of towner's. Marcus ate lunch and slept most of the night so he could get an early morning start back to Illinois. He bid farewell to his mother and family and promised to see them soon. It was such a long ride back to Rockwood.

The time coming back was virtually the same as when he left Illinois, only the weather was more accommodating. He arrived back in Rockwood, Illinois a half day later at around 9:00 PM.

He called Betty and his friends and told them he was back and had a safe trip. He went to bed early that night because he had to get up at 6:00 AM to get to work at 7:00 AM, plus pick up Betty in the process. Betty doesn't drive a car because of an accident that transpired years ago, leaving her with limited mobility. Betty is a native of Rockwood, Illinois, meeting Marcus at Dan's diner a couple of years ago. She's never been married and looks after her aging parents also living in Rockwood. Recently she was hired as a janitor at the college, same as Marcus. Her brothers and sisters are scattered throughout the states, so the sole responsibility falls on Betty in regards to the care of her parents. But everything seems to be working out okay.

Wednesday is "Pinochle Night" at the Rockwood Apartments at 7:00 PM. Sue and her mother, Jane, Rich, Bob and Eva, George and his wife Mary all join in. As we speak Marcus and Betty enter the recreation Parlor to join in the fun. No one plays cards for money or else some of the players will walk out poorer than they were when they came in. So its all for fun.

Sue and Jane inquired, "Marcus, how was your night trip to St. Louis? Was there a lot of traffic that late at night? How was the weather on your way up there? We were all praying for you." Marcus said, "The trip was fine. I stopped several times for coffee and breakfast."

Before the two tables of Pinochle got started, Sue remembered it was her and Jane's turn to provide the refreshments for the night. Jane started making the coffee and Sue brought the chocolate chip cookies into the recreation parlor and set them on the table. As they all sat at their tables visiting, munching on cookies, sipping steaming coffee and trying to concentrate on their cards, a large clap of thunder jolted everybody out of their chair. Rich said, "A storm must be moving into Rockwood. Does anybody have a radio? Marcus, how about you? Marcus said, "I left my radio at home and Betty doesn't have her radio either, because we usually listen to my car radio, sorry."

As they were surveying the situation, another clap of thunder shook the walls while a bolt of lightening struck the electrical power transformer and the electricity in the whole Rockwood Apartment building went out. George walked to the window to look outside and there wasn't a light to be seen, everything was dark and eerie looking. Jane said, "It might be hours before the electrical company restores power to the apartment complex."

She reached into her purse and found a small flashlight which she used to lead the tenants to their apartments so they wouldn't stumble and fall in the dark. After they were all safe in their apartments she led Marcus and Betty to their car and then she and Sue went to their own apartment and got out the candles like everybody else.

Sue said, "Mother, I'm sure happy that you had that flashlight in your purse, even though it was small, it came in handy." Jane said, "I always carry that with me out of habit, but this is the first time I've actually used it for a long time."

"Good for you, smart thinking." said Sue.

# CHAPTER 8
# ANOTHER MURDER

Occasionally on Friday nights, the Rockwood Apartment Complex has a pot luck supper for anybody that's willing to bring a dish, a healthy appetite and a desire to join in the fun. About thirty people got together for an enjoyable evening eating their favorite foods, playing cards, engaging in good conversation and making new friends. An inexpensive night out sharing a meal plus interesting company.

The evening was warm, October 8th to be exact, as the air conditioning was humming full blast. It had reached 93 degrees by five o'clock with very intense burning heat and with not a rain cloud in the sky. Everybody was bringing in their pot luck dish for supper as tables were set up in the recreation parlor with a vase of flowers adorning each table. A big pot of coffee was brewing on the counter, plus a large container of ice tea for the tea drinkers. Everybody furnished their own plates and silverware. As the tenants were filing in, several made comments about certain friends they were waiting for.

Friends they hadn't seen for a week or so, in spite of the close proximity of the apartment complex. Inquisitively Rich asked, "Has anyone seen George and Mary Sloan? They usually come down for these pot luck suppers. I think they've been to everyone that we've had so far." Bob commented, "The last time I saw him was this morning. He opened his apartment door the same time I did to get the morning paper; we exchanged our morning greetings and then closed our apartment doors. I haven't seen him since then."

"They'll probably walk in here any minute now."

A new billiard table had been added to the recreation parlor as Rich and Bob played a round of billiards with Rich winning so far. As the game comes to an end more tenants are taking their place at the table for a few minutes before they got in line for supper.

Sue excused herself from the pot luck supper tonight, since she is spending the night at her lady friends house that she is employed with at the Murphy Finance Company. Her mother, Jane, said, "I will be down a little later because I have several things to do first."

At this point, everybody is going past the long table picking up their food and eating themselves. Rich said grace and then everybody began to eat. As the tenants were eating and conversing the conversation gradually turned to George and Mary Sloan again. Rich said, "I inquired earlier in the evening where George and Mary Sloan were, but no one seemed to know, so I dropped the subject. Rich had no sooner said these words than the loud speaker started blaring an alert. Mr. Phillips was announcing the following, "There has been a murder and robbery in the elevator lobby about forty-five minutes ago. Mr. George Sloan was on his was down to the pot luck supper when he was shot in the head and passed away. Please discontinue what you are doing and leave the apartment complex immediately to Dan's Diner across the street, where you will be safe until further notification. Walk single file please. Dan's Diner is aware of what happened, so there is no need for an explanation. The Rockwood Police are at the complex as we speak, to inspect the building to make sure the killer is out of the building. Please leave now!"

The tenants jumped to their feet and gathered their few belongings together and walked single file across the street to Dan's Diner. As they sat in the booths and some at the lunch counter, discussing the evening's events, amidst mounds of smoked cigarettes, gallons of hot steaming coffee, the sounds of several tenants crying out loud and some softly weeping to themselves. The remainder of the tenants that were not at the pot luck supper also came into the diner as a precaution until further notice. The diner was full, as other customers came to the door and had to leave. A closed sign was put in the window and the curtains were drawn.

Finally at 10:00 PM the Rockwood Police came into the diner and told them "It is safe to go back into the complex, because we didn't find anything unusual at the apartments. Thank you." All sixty three of the tenants walked in groups across the street into the apartment building.

The next morning when everybody came into the main lobby Mr. Phillips had posted a notice on the bulletin board that there would be a meeting that night at 7:00 PM at the recreation parlor for all the tenants. A policeman would also be present at the meeting for questions and answers. Everybody was planning to attend.

As 7:00 PM approached that night the recreation parlor was filled with all the tenants that live at the complex, plus Marcus and Betty. They read about everything in the local paper and decided to attend. Mr. Phillips introduced Officer Green to the tenants and then proceeded with the meeting. After talking to Mary Sloan Mr. Phillips recounted the murder in this respect. "George and Mary Sloan were in the elevator, enroute to the recreation parlor for the pot luck supper, with Mary carrying a bowl of potato salad, when someone held the elevator door open and slipped inside before it shut. They were totally disguised, even their voice. Mary couldn't tell if it was a man or woman because their voice was low and gravely. He wore long dark pants, a vest and a scarf around his head and gloves. The scarf around his head was so you couldn't see his hair and a mask on his face. The voice could've been a man's yet it almost sounded like a woman's. They asked George for all the money he had with him and George said he only had a couple of dollars on him. This lack of so little money aggravated the killer, that George was shot execution style, facing Mary. Mary screamed as blood began pouring down his face and onto the carpet. The killer shot a bullet into each of George's eyes, which caused the eyes to fall out of their sockets and onto the elevator floor. Another bullet hit his head, exploding it, and exposing the brains. Blood and brains were seeping down the wall in tiny rivulets like a stream. The killer fired several more bullets into George's neck before he fled the elevator, detaching his head as it dropped on the elevator carpet. George's head rolled against the wall, as he bled profusely from his neck, exposing tissue, organs, arteries and veins. His dismembered body lay on the floor, as his eyeless head rolled from side to side. Both his brown eyes were lying on the floor next to his upper and lower torso which was still intact. Mary ran screaming out into the hall, "Help me! Help me! George has been shot," as the killer fled the elevator and out the side door of the complex. George was unable to speak anymore as his eyes closed in death. Mary knelt by his side holding his hand and weeping till the paramedics came to take him to the hospital. Mr. Phillips notified the next of kin and they were preparing to make the trip back to Rockwood, Illinois for the funeral and to be with their mother.

After a recount of the murder Officer Green answered questions as they were asked in regards to extra protection at the apartment complex, inside and out. Officer Green said, "Yes, we will be putting on extra duty policemen for the daytime and nighttime shift. We will also have a patrol car canvass the area periodically throughout the day and night for anything that looks suspicious or questionable to the police department. We will also have a policeman check the inside of the apartment complex to make sure everything is okay. Always feel free to call us if you have any problems. That's what we're here for. Our number is 501-234-2460. Thank you." The meeting adjourned for the evening and everyone went on home. Another meeting date will be set later on.

George Sloan was taken to Rockwood Hospital to confirm his death on paper and then transferred to the Brown Morgue for the final preparations.

## Thursday Afternoon, October 1999

George Sloan's two children came today to pay their respects to their father. Joe and his family came from East St. Louis, Missouri and Alice and her family came from Chicago, Illinois. Funeral services are not pending because the immediate family of George Sloan is here. The service will be Saturday morning at 10:00 AM at Brown's Mortuary followed by military honors at the cemetery. The casket will remain closed. In the evening Joe and Alice try to calm his mother, Mary, as she continuously weeps and laments the loss of her husband, George. As the evening wore on Mary isn't getting any better emotionally, so Joe and Alice decided to take Mary to the emergency room at Rockwood Hospital for an injection. Dr. Fulton gave Mary a dose of medication and then released her with some pills to calm her down. Gradually Mary became in control of her self again with the help of medication and an injection.

The funeral service for George Sloan is Saturday at 10:00 AM at the Brown Mortuary. The casket remains closed, adorned with a beautiful spray of flowers on top and surrounding the casket. A framed photograph of George graces the small table with a candle next to the casket.

Friends and relatives of the family are beginning to file in and proceed to the casket, many of them lingering to look at 82 year old Georges' photograph. The man they once knew, a vibrant, friendly, lovable human being now shrouded in death by the hand of a yet unbeknown source, either man or woman, still at large. The continuous search has turned up neither.

Pastor Jones of the Evangelical Baptist Church is conducting the service amidst weeping and sniffles among family, relatives, and friends. He gave a befitting eulogy about George and said various prayers. In conclusion they all sang two verses of an uplifting song, "When I come home," and they followed the casket out.

Everybody got in their cars and drove to Rockwood Cemetery for the internment of George Sloan. An opening for a grave was dug and Georges' casket was placed on top. Prayers were said and the military part of the funeral was conducted. Three shots were fired and then Taps were played to bring the funeral to a conclusion.

Before everybody left Pastor Jones said, "Everybody is invited for lunch in the basement of the Evangelical Baptist Church on 9th and Tyler St. back door entrance. Please come for good nourishing food and fellowship. See you there in a few minutes." Everybody left except

BLOOD SUCKING SERIES NO. 1: THE FINAL FLOOR

the immediate family which lingered for a little while, talking to the pastor and exchanging handshakes. Finally they all left the cemetery. On the way back to the church Alice said, "Mother, I'm so proud of you, you've regained your composure and are doing much better." Mary replied, "Thank you, Alice, I do feel much better than I did earlier. I know it will all take time."

Everybody went to the basement of the Evangelical Baptist Church on 9th and Tyler St. for lunch and visiting with one another. Some families hadn't seen each other for years, so there was almost more visiting than there was eating.

The next day Joe and Alice went back to their homes and Mary was left to fend for herself. She could always keep in touch by mail or phone or even go and see them by bus. She was due for a visit to both of them anyway. Besides she always had her friends there at the Rockwood Apartment Complex. Very good friends in fact.

Once a week Mary drives out to the Rockwood Cemetery to put fresh flowers on George's grave. Most of the time Mary spends weeping by the grave in spite of taking her medicine. As she said, "time heals all wounds."

Fall is fast approaching as the nights are getting cooler and crisp, typical jacket weather. Since it is getting cooler, only a few people can be seen out on the streets at night because of the change in weather, but also because of the danger that might lurk around any corner, since George was shot in the elevator. This was the third murder that has been committed in the last couple of years.

Officer Green and Officer Leeds are on the night shift together patrolling the area of the Rockwood Complex, even going inside and sometimes talking to the tenants saying, "Have you been experiencing anything suspicious or unusual lately, Rich? How about you, Bob? Have there been any strange people hanging around or sleeping on the blue couch in the recreation parlor?" You know, you're supposed to call the police department if you see anything different, Okay?"

"Are Marcus and Betty still coming around?" Asked Officer Leeds. "Not anymore said Bob." Not since he has a girlfriend now. He just comes and brings her along on Wednesday nights when we play cards.

Besides he has an apartment, not far from the college and a second hand car, so that's the only time he comes by."

"Okay, that's all we wanted to know then, remember what we said, Bye," said Officer Leeds and Officer Green.

A couple of days later they'll be back asking the same questions and getting the same answers. The killer is out for the time being. Like they say, "He's laying low for awhile and then gradually he'll surface again."

One evening Alex Bole, resident of the apartment complex, decided to walk downtown to the local pharmacy to buy some medication for himself. While he was browsing through the pharmacy he got thirsty and decided to slip into a booth for a coke and read the local paper a bit. While he was sitting there time got away from him. By this time it was totally dark, and he decided he'd better get back to the apartment complex. The weather was accommodating, crisp and cool, but never the less comfortable. After he had walked about two blocks he thought he heard a slight noise behind him, so he began to walk faster. The faster he walked, the faster the shuffle behind him, but he never looked back. He was too scared to by this time.

Finally after a couple of blocks of this, he decided to turn around. He didn't see anybody, so he continued walking. All of a sudden the shuffle got louder and he looked back and someone was chasing him. He started running full speed ahead but the person was right on his heels. As he came closer he shoved Alex in his back with both hands and he fell on the sidewalk all scratched up and bruised. The man yelled back at Alex, "Hah! I got you this time! You stupid fool." Alex yelled back, "I'll get you for this because I'm calling the police." The person rounded the corner and was long out of sight as Alex stumbled into the apartment complex telling everybody what had happened to him.

He immediately called the police, as Officer Green and Officer Leeds were patrolling in the vicinity of the apartments so they stopped in and talked to Alex. They interviewed him, and asked him numerous questions to be answered to the best of his ability, especially if he thought he would recognize this person in a police line up and he said he wasn't sure, because it was so dark and he fell on the sidewalk. Officer Leeds said, "If by chance this happens again try and get a better look at him." Alex said, "It probably won't happen again."

Officer Green interviewed him by asking, "Did you ever see this man before?" Alex said, "No, but it was too dark to get a good look at him." Officer Green asked him, "Can you give us a description of him to the best of your knowledge?" Alex said, "Not really, but I do remember that he wasn't tall, on the slim side and very fast. Again Officer Green asked him, "Did he have an accent, foreign or otherwise?" Alex replied, "No, I don't think so."

Officer Leeds and Officer Green said they'd leave now and if Bob thinks of any extra information that pertains to the incident, please contact the police department. They said they were going to check their police line up and other miscellaneous offenders.

When Officer Leeds and Officer Green got back to the police station they tried to match the offenders up with incidents such as Alex, but nothing seemed to work. They might have to wait till more complaints come in about him. Alex said, "That's the last time I'll walk to town at night by myself and get caught in the dark coming back. No more of that stuff. I'll order my medicine over the phone and have it delivered. It's getting so bad you can't walk to town and back without getting attacked." Everybody agreed and decided to do the same. It just wasn't worth taking a chance, unless there were several tenants from the apartments walking in a group. You know what they say, "There's safety in numbers."

Alex also made the remark, "Pretty soon it'll be too cold and dark to even be out walking such a long stretch from the apartments to downtown. I'd rather be inside where it's nice, warm and safe."

# Chapter 9
# Looking for the Killer

The Rockwood Police have never given up on their attempt to catch the killer of Fern Taylor, Bob Cain, and George Sloan, residents of the Rockwood Apartment Complex. Every time a new lead or clue surfaces they are on all three cases over and over again, but to no avail. Everything seems to disappear into thin air.

Similar crimes in other cities have been directed to the Rockwood Police Department to see if there is a connection between the murders. So far this has never been the case. Law enforcement officers from other cities have been assisting, plus the sheriff's and the Illinois FBI. They have combed the city and talked to various people, but nothing seems to materialize. They are all dead ends.

Periodically, the local Police Department organizes a group of people that want to span the hills countryside and surrounding area in search of any leads or clues that might have surfaced or possibly went unnoticed.

Sunday afternoon, a group of people congregated on the edge of town, at the base of the Blue Hills to help in the search for more clues to the recent killings. The coordinator of the search, Mr. Black, designated an area for everyone to start. A small group from the Rockwood Apartment Complex was gathered at the farther corner awaiting his designation.

## BLOOD SUCKING SERIES NO. 1: THE FINAL FLOOR

Mr. Black said, "Rich, Dave and you start at the base of the hill and work your way upward. Be careful. Joe and Jim, start at this end and work your way over to this area. Gerald and Dick, head over into the wooded part. Sue and Jane, come with me to another section. Marcus and Betty were searching also. I need to give further instructions to these other people. Its one thirty right now. I want this search party to meet back here at four o'clock. Don't be late. If you see anything unusual don't touch anything or poke around with your walking sticks as this can destroy vital evidence. Report any of your findings when you come back. Last chance for water, anybody want a drink? I see some of you brought your bottled water along. Okay, everybody divide into pairs and take off. My wife and I will go this way. Any questions? Let's go!"

Everybody dispersed in all directions. Two this way and two that way until they are all fielded out. As they were walking Bob said, "Rich, are you able to walk up this hill? It's getting a little steep." Rich replied, "I'm fine, I've done this many times when I was younger. It doesn't bother me now either. My knees have always been in good shape. I'm glad of that. I think we're two of the better ones out here from the Rockwood Apartment Complex, besides Sue and Jane. What do you think?" Rich said, "I think you're right. Everybody here today seems slower than you and I, with the exception of Sue and Jane. Some of these other men here today are almost to the point where they either need a walker or cane and probably a wheelchair later on. That's sad; I hope it'll never be you and I. "So do I", said Carl.

As they kept walking Rich made the remark, "I haven't seen anything unusual since we're scouring the area. Have you? We've come quite a distance out from where we started. Maybe we should turn around and go back now. Its 3:30 already and Mr. Black wants us to meet back at 4:00."

"Okay", said Carl, let's head back." They started walking north, but they came to a fence they hadn't encountered before. Rich said, "I didn't see this fence before, did you? I think we're walking the wrong way. Let's turn around and go back. There's still time."

"Okay", said Carl, we need to walk to the west now. We just walked the wrong way, that's all. It's got to be either west, north, east or south. Those are the only directions God made, so it's got to be one of them. Ready?"

Rich and Carl walked west for a little while, only to discover it was not the right way either. By this time it was 4:30 PM and they were already a half an hour late, but they knew that the search party wouldn't leave without them.

So they decided they would walk to the east, because surely this had to be the right way. The longer they walked east, the less they recognized having been on that path before. They even passed a small creek in the deeper wooded area they had never passed before. By this time it was getting to be dusk and small nocturnal animals were beginning to come above ground, out of the woods and the creek bed area to scamper and romp freely among the foliage and trees.

It was around 5:30 PM and Rich and Carl were now walking south as a last resort. The weather had turned cooler, cloudy and a slight mist has started to infiltrate the night air. Luckily they both had jackets on to protect themselves from the elements.

The farther they walked, the more lost they seemed to become. Rich remarked, "Carl what on earth are we going to do tonight? We will never get back because it's too dark and dangerous. I'm tired of walking and I'm beginning to get a bad cough from this damp air." Neither Rich nor Carl had their medication with them for the night, so they would have to do without.

Rich said, "I guess we'll just have to sit under some trees tonight till morning so we don't get too wet. Carl, I just can't figure out where we made the wrong turn when we were heading back to our search party. Do you know where we made the mistake?"

Carl said, "No, I don't know where we went wrong, but I'm sure glad we brought our flashlights and some snacks and bottled water. That will carry us over till morning, although I'm sure neither you nor I will sleep a wink tonight."

As Carl and Rich were walking south through the woods, they came upon a clearing void of all foliage and trees with a small, dilapidated,

*BLOOD SUCKING SERIES NO. 1: THE FINAL FLOOR*

wooden shack setting there. They opened the door and went inside and found too wooden cots, a little bedding and a table and two chairs. There was no electricity, running water and no bathroom. Carl said, jokingly, "Well, it isn't exactly the Hilton Hotel, but it's good enough for the night. At least we have a roof over our heads, and a place to sleep tonight, that is if we can sleep. I don't think I can under this extreme situation. Do you think you will be able to nod off tonight Rich?"

Rich said, "You know I can't. Carl, I feel bad because we were so foolish and lost our way. We should've been more conscientious about the path we took when we left the Blue Hills, remember? How are we going to get back tomorrow? I know everybody is worried about us. No one is going to think of us in this secluded area of all places. I can't believe this is happening to us. Can you?"

Carl commented, "Well, it's too late now. It's water under the bridge and we can't do anything about that now except pray that someone will rescue us tomorrow."

Rich said, "I'm one step ahead of you. I already prayed. Goodnight."

"Goodnight," said Carl.

Naturally, Rich and Carl awoke bright and early to a sun filled morning with birds chirping and the nocturnal animals still scampering around looking for food. Rich and Carl were the same as their nocturnal animal friends, looking for food. "No bacon and eggs or pancakes with coffee this morning," said Rich. "That's right," said Carl, We'll each have a granola bar and a bottle of water. Some breakfast! Huh! I'm so hungry I could eat a bear. Have you seen one running by?" Carl said, "No, but I'm sure they are in the area somewhere. I wouldn't want to be out by myself at night out here. It's too dangerous."

"Well, let get down to basics, said Rich and figure this whole mess out." We don't have our cell phones with us, but we do have our transistor radios. Let's turn on RCWD 1700 in Rockwood. There it is with country music playing all day. I like that station. Let's listen to the news now for a change."

"Okay," said Carl, but sometimes it gets kind of boring because it's the same old news, nothing different. Just a minute, what's that? There talking about us, Rich."

"What are you talking about?' said Rich. The radio announcer was giving the ten o'clock Monday morning news as follows: "A massive search with canines is underway at present for two men from the Rockwood Apartment Complex by the names of Rich Burns and Carl Biller, last seen yesterday afternoon. Both men were part of a search party that is conducted every four months to assist in the whereabouts of the recent killer of George Sloan. They were last seen around 2:00 PM yesterday afternoon headed for the Blue Hills. When Mr. Black had the search party meet back at 4:00 PM Rich and Carl did not report back with the rest of the searchers. Once again, I repeat, a massive hunt with canines has been underway since 6:00 AM this morning, but nothing has turned up so far. The city of Rockwood has two helicopters circling in the area near the Blue Hills where Rich and Carl were last seen.

If you are listening to this broadcast this morning please stand in an open area, scream and raise your arms and wave, so you can readily be seen and identified and we will pick you up."

Rich and Carl immediately heard a whirring noise. As they looked up they saw a helicopter whirring around overhead. They both yelled and flailed their arms to draw attention to themselves and they were seen.

The helicopter landed in the clearing and Rich and Carl climbed in and were taken back to Rockwood City. Enroute on the flight back Rich and Carl explained to the pilot, Mr. Sand, the circumstances of their disappearance. The pilot said, "You were lucky you got rescued today because there are a lot of wild nocturnal animals out at night and it's extremely dangerous."

The pilots said, "Both of you were pictured in the local paper today and an "all points" bulletin was released by the Rockwood Police Department in the event that you would be seen and recognized."

The pilot radioed back to the Rockwood Apartment Complex and told them he was bringing Rich and Carl back safe and sound.

There was no time for the welcoming committee to put on a display, so they rejoiced with Rich and Carl when they entered the complex and told everybody how good it was to be back with their friends again. They proceeded to give the details of their disappearance and answered various questions that were asked. The next day, Tuesday afternoon, would be a formal welcome reception for them, inviting the residents of The Rockwood Complex and the public within the city of Rockwood.

The next afternoon, Tuesday, at 2:00PM the recreation parlor, lobby, hallways and extra rooms were overflowing with the apartment residents and well wishers bestowing their good wishes on them and telling them they were in many people's prayers and that God was with them.

Rich and Carl spoke at different intervals during the reception, thanking the residents and numerous other well wishers for their prayers and out pouring of love and kindness during their absence from their friends. Rich and Carl stood on either side of the door shaking hands with everybody and thanking them for coming and hoping to see them soon. Mr. Black the coordinator for the search party came by to shake hands with Rich and Carl and to exchange a few words. Mr. Black said, "The search party waited an extra hour for you and when you didn't show up everyone went back home. I immediately called the Rockwood Police Department and a search party was organized Sunday night after the group got back. It was called off at 10:00 PM when people were spanning the hills with walking sticks, flashlights and calling their names, to which there was no answer. They resumed the search Monday morning again and then was called off because both of you had been located. Everybody's glad it had a happy ending. Mr. Black asked them, "Have you ever been able to figure out which direction you walked by mistake?" Carl and Rich said, "No, not yet, and laughed it off. Mr. Black said, "The search party was not confronted with anything different or unusual, anymore than they were other times when we searched the country side. They're were no clues or leads to anything different. Nothing to report back to me. George Sloan's killer could be out of the state and across the country by now, for all we know. And then again, on the other hand, he could be right here in our midst, and we would be none the wiser. No one knows for sure, but God."

## Several Weeks Later...

Lately, several people from the apartment complex have reported sightings of a transit by himself. Lurking in the lobby and recreation parlor after normal business hours on any given day. He doesn't converse with anybody, watches the men play billiards, drinks coffee and watches TV. Occasionally, he reads the newspaper and when it's dinner or suppertime he leaves. Several people have asked him what his name is and he says, "My name is Alvin Rindle." He doesn't volunteer any information about himself. It seems like he's replacing Marcus since Marcus doesn't hang around the apartments anymore, because he has an apartment of his own now.

Alvin is short in height, thin, long dark hair, about 35 years old and slovenly dressed. He has a knapsack strapped to his back for his personal belongings. He never sleeps in the recreation parlor where Marcus used to sleep, on the blue divan, but leaves around 10:00 PM. He's another person similar to Marcus though. Mr. Phillips, the land lord, said "Just let him go, because he isn't harming anyone and doesn't stay overnight. He's just another homeless person. Where do they all come from? Off the highway, no doubt."

One afternoon Alex, the man who was chased and pushed in the back while walking home from town one night, was sitting in the recreation parlor, reading the newspaper. Alvin Rindle was sitting across from him, watching TV. Alex looked at him several times thinking, "Where did I see this guy before? He sure looks familiar." Alex kept studying his face, yet he couldn't place him. So he tried to engage Alvin in a conversation and it worked. Alex recognized the voice immediately. It was the same voice that yelled these words at Alex after he shoved him walking home from downtown onto the snowy sidewalk. He said, "Hah! I got you, you stupid fool." Alex yelled back, "I'll get you for this because I'm going to call the police." Well, now was his chance. He excused himself and said he'd be right back. Alex went to his apartment and told his wife Stella what had happened, and she also suggested calling the police which he did.

Officer Green and Officer Leeds came within a few minutes up to the apartment complex, and questioned Alvin Rindle. He couldn't deny it because the police had booked him for other minor offenses several years ago. So he signed an admission of guilt paper and they handcuffed him and led him away.

# CHAPTER 10
## DETECTIVES ON CALL

As soon as it became common knowledge about the murders taking place in the elevator at the Rockwood Apartment Complex, detectives from various areas were called to assist in certain departments. They came from as far away as St. Louis, Missouri and as close as Bixby and Plattsville, Illinois.

After the murder of Fern Taylor numerous detectives were called to Rockwood, Illinois. They spent several days in conferences and meetings before spanning the hills and countryside to look for clues and leads as to the whereabouts of the killer or killers.

All detectives were referred to the Diamond Motel on the edge of town for the duration of time they would be here. As they were unpacking Detective Lewis said to Detective Lee, "I wonder if we will find any clues or leads north of Interstate 70 because that's a pretty desolate area. I doubt it, but we have to canvas everything, regardless."

Detective Lee said, "Whoever committed Fern Taylor's murder could be across the country by now, probably in another state. I doubt if we'll ever find him."

Detective Lewis said, "That's what I think."

The next morning, which was Monday, Detectives Lewis and Lee proceeded to check Fern's personal belongings and her most recent phone bill for new and unusual telephone calls. They also visited with Fern's friends at the complex and whose names she mentioned often. Did she have any enemies that they knew of? Did she have any friends at Dan's diner that she frequented every morning? After they compiled there answers in a notebook, which took a good part of the day, they proceeded to Dan's Diner for further investigation. The detectives asked Dan, the owner, "How often and what time of the day did Fern Taylor come into the diner and with whom and did she always sit by herself?" A couple of times an older man from another booth came and sat with her. Dan said he didn't know the older man, but he wasn't from the Rockwood Complex. Dan said, "I'm sure there's a simple explanation for that."

While Dan was talking to the detectives, the older man that sat with Fern Taylor several times came walking into the diner for an occasional cup of coffee. Dan waited on him in the booth and said, "The detectives want to talk to you." He said, "Okay." Detectives Lewis and Lee climbed into the booth and introduced themselves and asked him what his name was and about Fern Taylor. He said, "My name is John Block and I've know Fern for years. In fact, we both went to the same school and both of us are natives of Rockwood. Fern's about ten years older than I am. She even knew my wife years ago, although she's passed away now."

The detectives inquired about Fern Taylor's family. Detective Lee asked, "Did Fern have any brothers or sisters?" John replied, "Yes, she had one brother by the name of Steve Taylor and three sisters, two living in Denver, Colorado and the other sister living in outer Montana. Steve Taylor was in my class at school."

When Detectives Lewis and Lee were satisfied with their answers, they thanked Mr. Block for his information and hoped they hadn't imposed on him.

By this time Detectives Lee and Lewis were getting hungry, as it was close to supper time, so they decided to eat at the diner.

After they were done eating they drove back to the Diamond Motel on the edge of town, ready to retire.

The next morning after breakfast at Dan's Diner, they proceeded to check out the different businesses that Fern frequented. Places such as her church, the food market, variety stores and other places of interest. Everything met their expectations, so they went back to the Diamond Motel.

The next morning Detectives Lee and Lewis spanned the woods and hills and called for "back up" detectives, as it was quite an area to cover. When the "back up" detectives came they covered the complete area, but to no avail, because everything was the same as it was before.

The detectives went back to St. Louis, Missouri and two new detectives would be coming in the near future.

One Month Later...

Detective Blount and Detective Still were sent to Rockwood, Illinois to check out the murder of Bob Cain in the elevator. Did any new clues or leads surface? After Bob Cains death different places of interest were checked out and they all proved negative.

Detectives Still and Blount visited with Mrs. Cain, but it just reopened fresh wounds, so they didn't pressure her any longer. Detective Still asked, "Did you have any enemies that would do such a thing and she said, "No, not that she knew of."

Detective Jones worked on the case immediately after the rattlesnake in the elevator struck Bob Cain in the chest and heart, taking his life at 8:42 PM, upon arrival at the hospital.

Detectives Still and Blount are searching for clues, leads, names, suspicious characters, anything to solve the case, but to no avail. This afternoon they interviewed many of the residents of the Rockwood Apartments to see if they remembered or saw anything being carried into the lobby or the elevator itself. Or perhaps a large box setting in the lobby that could conceal a 6 ft rattlesnake. Everybody wracked their brains, but nobody could come up with anything, nor did anybody notice or see anybody or anything unusual that day. No one can account for the times when the lobby and elevator were both empty, especially after hours. Anybody could have gone in and set a box in the elevator and opened the lid.

The snake would've crawled out of the box, lay in the elevator in full view and attacked Bob Cain when he entered the elevator, striking him in the chest and heart.

But the sixty-four dollar question is, "How did the snake get into the elevator? Someone had to bring him in a sealed container. There's no other way. Is this going to happen again? Who would do such an unimaginable thing and why? It seems like someone has a dislike for the residents of the Rockwood Apartment Complex. Why? What did they ever do to anybody?"

Three Months Later…

Three months have passed since George Sloan was shot and killed in the elevator. Neither clues nor leads have surfaced since that fateful night this past August.

Detective Jones is working on this case with the Rockwood Police Department, and as of to date nothing has turned up. He has interviewed all of the apartment tenants about old and new people coming and going at different times of the day and night, but everything seems normal. As far as anybody lurking outside the Rockwood Apartment Complex, nothing has been reported, as police have been patrolling the area for years, ever since the killings began. Except there is one person…Alvin Rindle.

Alvin Rindle was handcuffed and taken to jail for attacking Alex Bole on the way home from downtown one night, pushing him onto the snowy sidewalk. He then ran off yelling snide remarks and left him limping to the apartment complex.

Alvin Rindle had been lounging around in the lobby for a month or two until Alex spoke to him and recognized his voice and called the police.

Detective Jones interviewed him about George Sloan's murder and used a lie detector test on him which was negative. All the suspects in jail have been interviewed, and statements made, finger printed, and a lie detector test used on them in regard to the three killings at the Rockwood Apartment Complex and they all proved negative. At this point the killer has supposedly eluded the police department and has failed to come forth after an extensive and futile search. We will continue in our effort to bring forth the killer.

Alvin Rindle was acquitted of all three murders committed at the Rockwood Apartment Complex, namely Fern Taylor, Bob Cain and George Sloan. But, he was guilty of attacking Alex Bole on his way home from downtown one night and is serving time in jail for that offense.

## December

On a cold, snow packed, winter night in the beginning of December sirens could be heard blaring all through the city of Rockwood, alerting people of a city wide chase by the Rockwood Police Department in response to a break in for murder and domestic dispute.

As it turned out the Rockwood Service Station on Brown St. was robbed and two local attendants, Marie Bean and Joan Clum, were killed at gun point, after losing thousands of dollars in cash. The police chased the robbers at ninety miles per hour down Main St., headed south out of town. A road block was set up instantly, to which they detoured.

As one fugitive, John Bell, said to the other one, Dan Cone, "Why in the devil did you head south out of town? I told you they'd probably set up a road block on the main highway, and I was right. Slow down, dammit and let me out of here! I'm fleeing on foot. I never did want any part of this whole deal anyway. You talked me into it. Here's your lousy money. I hope they shoot your head off. That'll teach you a lesson, you stupid idiot."

Dan Cone replied, "Get the hell out of here and I never want to see you again. If the police capture me I'm still going to list you as an accomplice. So there, if our paths ever cross again you're not going to get one thin dime. OUT!" As John slowed down Dan jumped out, and scampered into the fields, limping and carrying his duffel bag, and swearing all the way. You stupid shit! I hope I never see you again as long as I live!"

Dan Cone continued on his way out of town, as John Bell scurried into the fields completely out of sight by now.

Later, he could be seen hitch hiking into Rockwood by way of the back roads while Dan continued on his way out of town, trying to avoid the police. John Bell and Dan Cone were eventually captured and brought to the Rockwood Police Station for questioning about the service station robbery and shootings and the murders at the Rockwood Apartment Complex, amongst other petty thefts.

Their finger prints didn't match any of the finger prints on record. The lie detector test and questioning both proved negative, so the detectives had no choice but to dismiss them. Since it was snowing when they left, the police referred them to a homeless shelter for men.

A Week Later...

Recently, reports have filtered into the Rockwood Police Department from the Rockwood Apartment Complex about possible sightings of unsavory characters lurking inside and outside the apartment complex on any given day or night. Discarded cigarettes, paper wrappers and odds and ends have been seen strewn outside the apartment windows on the lower floor.

Several of the residents saw a man's face stare in the window briefly and then disappear, unrecognizable to anyone.

At any time, there are unidentifiable characters in the recreation parlor using it as a safe haven to relax remove themselves from inclement weather, watch a little television, and possibly spend the night on the blue divan.

On this particular night more sightings were seen than usual, which prompted a visit from the police department.

Detectives Still and Blount have interviewed the residents at length and everybody came up with the same description. A dark haired, forty-five year old man has been seen on different occasions staring in the ground floor windows, and then stepping away. The detectives have been posting themselves outside the complex windows unnoticed, while other detectives have been driving by periodically.

One evening as they were driving by, they saw a man staring in the apartment windows and Detective Blount flashed his car lights on him and yelled. "What are you doing over there?" The man answered, "None of your damn business," and ran across the street behind a building to elude the police. They stopped their car and chased him on foot for several blocks until they caught him coming around the building the wrong way. He tried to run the opposite way, but they caught him and took him to the police station. They asked him, "What's your name?" To which he answered, "Tom Logan."

"Why were you looking in the windows of the apartments?"

"Oh, I don't know, just to see if I knew anybody. I didn't mean anything by it. I won't do it anymore."

The police said, "You'd better not because you've been reported to the police department on different occasions. We'd better not see any more of that. We'll have to give you a fine and you'll have to spend several days in jail to teach you a lesson. Okay?" Mr. Logan agreed. "You'll be in cell number 2, over there."

"Tomorrow we have further issues to take up with you since you're a repeat offender. Its getting too late tonight, said Detective Blount.

The next morning they interviewed him, fingerprinted him and took a lie detector test, to which everything tested normal, in regards to the three murders at the Rockwood Apartment Complex. In several days he was released again with a close eye on him from the police department.

Upon his release Detective Blount remarked, "If we get anymore reports about you from anybody at all, you'll get a terrible fine that will take years to pay and on top of that, you'll be confined to jail for a year. Now get the damn hell out of here or I'll throw you out with my own bare hands. I don't want to see the likes of you anymore."

"OUT!"

## December 24, 2000

It's Christmas Eve and the city of Rockwood is aglow with sparkling Christmas lights; a soft snow falling and the last minute shoppers trudging homeward with their packages in tow. "Merry Christmas and Happy New Year" could be heard from shoppers up and down the streets. "Same to you," was the reply.

While down at the police station things were relatively quiet for a change, except for the police calling in periodically to give a report on their beat. About 9:30 PM an anonymous caller called the police department saying, "I'd like to report a body, lying face downward in some tall weeds about two hundred feet north of the green, slushy, murky Thunder Creek. The body was left untouched as I scrambled out of the tall weeds to report my findings to the police department." Detectives Still and Blount and several other policemen left immediately for Thunder Creek about 5 miles west of Rockwood, off of Highway 7.

As they approached Thunder Creek with their cars, an ambulance, search lights, flash lights and a gurney in their attempt to retrieve the body. Detective Still read this report to the other policemen. "Upon examination, we have found a young woman, about 30 years old, fully clothed, with a blue jacket, dark brown hair and eyes, light skinned, about 5 ft 5 inches tall, about 135 lbs lying face downward in some tall weeds about 200 feet north of Thunder Creek. Possibly a victim of a blow to the head with a sharp instrument. Basically, she was bludgeoned to death at the hands of her killer and left in the weeds."

There was no identification, nor recognition on the victim. It was impossible to identify her because of the level of decomposition the body had been exposed to and the trauma involved.

Brushing the snow off the body, they hoisted it on a gurney and wheeled it to the waiting ambulance attendees for the trip back to the Brown Mortuary.

The body was re-examined by several morticians and forensic experts and an autopsy was performed to rule out the ingestion of foreign substances. The autopsy was labeled routine and normal with no foreign matter inside the body. Death was attributed to a bludgeoning blow on the head by a blunt instrument. There was instant death as soon as the killer dealt the blow. She was immediately hand cuffed and hauled into the weeds, being left for dead. An unannounced visitor came past Thunder Creek, stumbled upon the body and reported it to the Rockwood Police Department.

Several days later the police department captured three men speeding and skidding on Interstate 70 past the town of Rockwood. They pulled them over and questioned them. Not satisfied with their answers they handcuffed all three of them and booked them into jail. After they interviewed them extensively, took fingerprints, and a lie detector test they released them because they were not associated with the Rockwood Apartment Complex murders, nor the body found at Thunder Creek.

Another murder left unsolved.

An Unusually Warm Day…

Still unsatisfied with the unusual deaths plaguing the city, Detectives Blount and Still and a few others decided to drag Thunder Creek in search of anything unusual pertaining to the murders in the city. Wearing clothing suitable for the watery search, they immersed their bodies in the tepid water and drug Thunder Creek with a seine from beginning to end in search of anything different at all. As they crawled out of the murky slimy water Detective Blount made the remark, "I kind of figured dragging Thunder Creek would be a waste of time, but you never know." We always have to exercise on the side of caution. Too many odd, strange things have been happening these last few years, beginning with Fern Taylor's death in 1995. I wonder if any of this will ever get solved. What do you think?" Detective Still said, "As far as I'm concerned, solving the murders at this point seems almost impossible. The killer is covering his tracks pretty good. We have no leads, clues, suspicious characters, nothing. I think we've reached a dead end. When we do get something that's promising, it seems like we're always barking up the wrong tree. Let's head on back to the motel, because I'm starving. How about you?" Detective Blount said, "I'm ready to go. I haven't eaten since breakfast. I'm hungry for a steak dinner. Let's get the hell out of here. It's kind of eerie anyway!"

As they were heading back to town, in the dark, they encountered two hitchhikers standing on the side of Interstate 70, their thumbs pointed west. Detective Blount and Still pulled off the Interstate and onto the shoulder of the highway, and questioned them. "Where are you headed?" asked Detective Blount. "We're headed for Denver, Colorado. We're hoping someone will stop and give us a ride," said the hitchhiker. "Could you give us a ride for any distance? My buddy and I are awfully tired. We've been standing here about an hour and no one has stopped and offered to give us a ride. We're also getting very hungry."

Detective Still said, "Detective Blount and I are detectives and we are not allowed to give hitchhikers a ride. Actually, you're not supposed to be hitchhiking this close to the city limits. If a policeman were to come by you would probably get a ticket, because this law just went into effect and they are really beginning to enforce it. And you could possibly go to jail overnight. You'd better be careful. My suggestion would be to walk another mile west and try to hitchhike from there."

Both hitchhikers said, "Thank you and goodbye." They were taking the detectives advice and headed another mile west for fear of getting a ticket or an overnight stay in jail.

Detective Blount and Detective Still went on to eat their steak dinner at the motel, watched a little television, and then retired for the evening, as they were both very tired.

The next morning at 6:00 AM, bright and early, both detectives were on their way back to St. Louis, Missouri to replace two other detectives that were headed to Rockwood, Illinois in search of the killer or killers.

# Chapter 11
# A New Maid

Meanwhile, as all these events unfolded, Marcus' girlfriend Betty is making herself available as a private maid at the Rockwood Apartments, because she quit her job as janitor at Rockwood College.

Currently, she is working for George Sloan's wife Mary in their 4$^{th}$ floor apartment. Mary doesn't like being by herself at night since her husband George was murdered. She would rather have someone stay with her at night, especially to answer the anonymous telephone calls late in the evening. Betty stays overnight with Mary Monday and Tuesday of every week, does a little cooking and cleaning, gets her medication at the pharmacy etc…, she comes to work at 7:00 AM on Monday and leaves at 7:00 AM on Wednesday.

She also works for Bob Cain's wife Ella, 84 years old, on Thursday and Fridays, but she doesn't stay overnight because Ella can stay by herself at night. Betty does the same thing for Ella as she does for Mary. Since Betty bought herself a car when she was employed as a janitor at Rockwood College, it's easer for her to get around. She takes Ella and Mary for a ride on Sunday, her day off, to break the monotony of the week, and Ella and Mary enjoy going. Betty quit working as janitor at the college because she said "Hell, this work is too hard, pushing a broom all day long and I get too tired because I never get to sit down.

*BLOOD SUCKING SERIES NO. 1: THE FINAL FLOOR*

I hate this damn janitorial work. Never again! I'm leaving this job the first chance I get." And leave she did! She applied for a job at the Rockwood Apartment Complex the same day she quit at Rockwood College and was hired immediately.

One day when Betty came to work she found Mary Sloan sitting on the divan sobbing her heart out. Walking over and putting her arm around her Betty said, "Mary, what's the matter? What Happened? Aren't you feeling well? Tell Betty all about it. I'm here for you." Mary kept on sobbing even louder than before, lamenting her plight in so many words. "Betty, do you know what happened to me?" Betty said, "Of course not, Mary. I'm in the apartment all day with you and then two days with Ella, so I don't hear much of anything else that goes on in the apartments, then I go home to my parents where I live. What's the matter? Are the anonymous calls coming when I'm not here? You need to tell me more about those calls in detail so we can report them to the police."

Mary replied, "Betty, it seems to me like someone knows the hours when you're here and gone, because the calls seem to coincide with your coming and going. I received a telephone call again Wednesday morning about 10:00 AM, a couple of hours after you left. Did you see any sleazy character in a phone booth when you left, Betty?"

Betty said, "No, I didn't Mary. Of course I didn't pay any particular attention to anything when I walked out of the apartment complex. I remember I said I was in a hurry to get home to my parents because my mother wasn't feeling well, so I moved right along." Mary said, "Yes, I remember you telling me that. Well, here's what happened. Like I said, a couple of hours after you left Wednesday morning, I was sitting here watching TV when the telephone rang. I picked it up and answered "Hello" several times and no one answered so I hung up. There was no sound at the other end of the line, just dead silence. About a half an hour later the telephone rang again, there was a moment of silence, while I caught my breath, then I heard a raspy voice at the other end of the line asking, "Is this Mary Sloan?"

To which I replied, "Yes, may I ask who's calling, please?" They said, "Yes, I do mind when you ask who's calling, because it's none of your damn business, and don't ever ask again, or you'll be sorry. You might be sorry the way it is."

Mary couldn't tell if it was a man or woman's voice. It sounded like it could be a man's voice, but on the other hand, when you listened a little longer it sounded like it could've been a woman's voice disguised. Mary did not recognize the voice as anyone she knew.

There was a dead silence again, and finally the anonymous caller said, "I wouldn't step into the elevator again if I were you, Mary. Remember what happened to your husband, George? George was a good, righteous, God fearing man, yet he was murdered."

By this time Mary was sobbing and fearing for her life because they were basically threatening her with murder again. The anonymous caller told Mary specifically, "Don't step into the elevator anymore or you might not live to tell about it." By this time Mary was beside herself with fear and panic and not holding up very well.

She pleaded with them to leave her alone repeatedly, but they wouldn't hear of it. If they wanted money she would give them that, but not her life. She only wanted to be left alone. She wanted her peace and quiet, like everybody else.

Betty suggested calling the police, but Mary wouldn't hear of it, because she said it would aggravate the caller even more. Mary has no intention of entering the elevator anymore, since she now takes the back stairs to the main lobby. It is harder for her to walk the stairs at her age, but she feels like she has no choice at this point.

Several Days Later…

After Betty is confronted with Mary's problem in regards to the anonymous caller, Ella, Bob Cains wife is experiencing the same dilemma. Ella has been receiving anonymous telephone calls from someone for the past several days telling her to stay out of the elevator or else she will go the same route as her husband Bob. Ella lives on the 4$^{th}$ floor down the hall from Mary.

Ella can't distinguish the caller from a man or woman because they sounded so alike, raspy and low pitched. She was weeping and feared for her life and the thought of the anonymous caller lurking in the Rockwood Apartment Complex left her panic sticken with fear.

She told Betty and she offered to call the police more than once, but Ella said no because she didn't want to make the situation any worse than it was already. Ella has taken the back stairs with Mary to the main lobby. It is very hard for her to walk the stairs at the age of 92, but it's better than having something happen to her in the elevator. She has no choice, for the time being.

Sometimes, in the evenings, Mary comes to Ella's apartment to visit, while Betty finishes the dishes, does light housework or goes to the pharmacy, since Mary is heavily medicated.

As Mary was saying, "Ella, I just can't figure this whole thing out. Isn't it strange that you and I have been singled out in this large apartment complex, so far, to be receiving these anonymous telephone calls? Is it just because our husbands were murdered in the main elevator or is it something else we're unaware of. I wish we knew. What do you think, Ella? Got any ideas? Aren't you scared? I know I am!"

Ella replied, "I don't know what to make of this whole mess and I'm getting sick and tired of everything by now. I wish that creep or creeps would stop harassing us and leave us alone. Its sad enough our husbands were murdered in the main elevator. We don't need these weird, sickening anonymous telephone calls to frighten us and keep us up half the night."

Mary agreed, making the remark, "I don't need this kind of a problem. I'm scared to stay by myself as it is since George is gone."

While Ella and Mary were visiting another telephone call broke the dead of silence. Ella answered, "Hello…Hello…Hello", and finally the caller said, "You two stupid old bitches, I'm gonna get you, one way or another. Wait and see." Ella cried into the phone, "Please, please, what did Mary and I ever do to you? We don't even know you. Who are you?"

The caller answered, "I've always hated older people. I'll never become old like you and a burden to other people. I'll see to that myself. And not only that you might be interested in knowing that I'm close to you, maybe just around the corner. You'd be surprised if you knew." Slam! The receiver went back on the hook leaving Ella and Mary crying and more fearful than ever.

By this time, Mary was ready to go back to her own apartment and face the rest of the day, besides watching a little television, visiting with Betty and then retiring for the night. It's been a long, harrowing day. Ella was very upset when Mary left, to the point, that she was also getting scared to stay by herself at night. Especially, since the caller said he was close at hand, like anyone wanted him around.

Mary told Betty about the telephone call at Ella's apartment and what the caller said, about being close at hand. Is he lurking in the Rockwood Complex somewhere? If so, where? Betty said, "I wasn't here at that time. I went to Byer's Pharmacy to get your prescription filled. I didn't see anything unusual when I left or came back, although sometimes I'm not too observant. Now just a minute, come to think of it, I did see an unfamiliar man leave the complex right at the time I came in the front door. He looked like a typical bum, grungy, a smelly appearance, unshaven, torn, tattered clothes, the whole works. I said "Good afternoon" and he grunted. I watched him as he walked north, down the street, headed towards downtown. That's the first time I've ever seen him here at the complex. He didn't look familiar to me.

I still think we should turn these telephone calls in to the Rockwood Police Department and let them work on this case. They can trace the telephone calls to the point of origin, wherever that may be. Or they could question the people here at the complex to see if anyone besides herself saw him or did anyone talk to him or recognize his voice from somewhere. He should be checked out because he could be a suspect. There are too many strange people coming and going at the complex anymore. What do you think, Mary?"

Mary said, "Oh, I don't know, I'm still not too fond of that idea. If the caller finds out that we called the police, he'll get mad for damn sure and you and I are liable to be victims of circumstances! That would be terrible. We're just plain scared." Betty said, "Well, Okay, I won't report anything till you tell me to."

Betty went home as usual on Wednesday night at 7:00PM to care for her ailing mother. Mary stays by herself the rest of the week at night. As she was sitting by herself that same night that Betty left, she heard a terrible banging on her apartment door, no voices, just an incessant banging which practically scared her to death. She was scared to answer the door, so she stood in the apartment and waited for the noise to subside and then she answered. There was no one in sight. The hallway was empty and everybody's apartment door was closed. She walked over to Ella's apartment door and knocked and Ella opened the door with a fearful, ashen look on her face as if something had scared her. Mary said, "Ella did somebody bang on your door about ten minutes ago?" Ella replied, "Yes, and I'm still scared. I didn't even want to open the door. Did someone bang on your door too, Mary?" Mary said, "Yes, that's why I finally came out into the hall to see what's going on. I wonder if it's the anonymous caller." Ella made the comment, "I think so, because I believe he's trying to scare us. I guess it's time we called the police because this is going a little bit too far. What do you think, Mary?" Mary agreed that it's time to call the police.

So, Ella and Mary called the police department and Officers Green and Leeds came out immediately and questioned Ella and Mary about everything that's been going on the past couple of weeks. They decided to post a policeman at the complex in case of unusual activity or disturbances.

There were no anonymous telephone calls or banging on the apartment doors for the next couple of weeks. Everything seemed just fine until one night later in the week Ella and Betty were awakened toward morning with a loud banging on their door at 5:00 AM which woke them up. They both opened their doors later, simultaneously, and each had a note left in their door saying, "I hope you have your funeral planned because you're going to need it." Ella and Mary cried bloody tears, as they again decided to call the police, even though it was 5:00 AM in the morning and they hated to bother them again. Officer Green and Leeds were there within ten minutes, consoling them and reassuring them they would get to the bottom of the matter. This very night they posted a policeman at each door for security purposes for Ella and

Mary and the rest of the complex, which they greatly appreciated. The policemen went home in the morning and two others took their place.

In the evening Ella and Mary decided to walk downtown to eat supper for a change. Mario's restaurant was full with a small seating capacity, but they were still going to wait. By the time they sat down to eat their steak dinner it was dark and the steak was cold. The waitress warmed their meal up in the microwave and Ella and Mary ate and left immediately because by now it was late. There are five blocks from Mario's restaurant to the Rockwood Apartment Complex. Everything was okay as they walked the first block. In the second block they heard someone's footsteps a little ways behind them. They both looked back and saw someone walking about a half block behind them. Now he's about a fourth of a block behind them. Ella and Mary are also picking up speed with only two blocks to walk. They look again and he's only one house away. They yell, "Get away from us, you sicko, leave us alone. Who are you anyway?" He laughed and said, "You'll know soon enough."

By this time, the reached the apartment complex, and hurriedly went inside. Ella and Mary peered out the window as the night stalker walked on.

In the meantime Officer Green and Leeds have been doing a little detective work on the anonymous telephone calls. They checked the downtown area with phone booths outside and were told from a local business that a woman was sitting in the phone booth at different times the night of the calls. Officer Green had a picture of Betty from the main lobby and the pharmacist happened to recognize her as the person that's making the calls to the apartment complex and banging on the apartment doors and leaving threatening notes.

The next day Officer Leeds and Green came to the apartments of Mary and Ella. Actually, they all met in Ella's apartment and the two policemen explained how the case is already solved and they don't have to be fearful anymore.

As Officer Leeds said, "Your maid, Betty, is the one that's been calling you on the phone and banging at your door and leaving notes. We checked it all out and we have proof of everything. We will get back to you later, as we are getting ready to go to her parents home where she lives to arrest her. Thank you!"

When they arrived at Betty's parent's home they were all sitting on the porch. Officer Leeds and Green approached her and explained the situation, handcuffed her and led her away. They asked her if she had anything to say to her parents and she said, "Yes, everything's true and I'm sorry for what I did. Please forgive me. I wished I would've never done this."

The police booked her in jail, a trial was held the following week and the judge sentenced her to two years in a women's prison in Plattsville, Illinois with no chance for parole. Marcus was unaware of what was going on and was very upset. Betty continues to apologize, but the damage is done.

Marcus, in spite of his anger, continues to visit her faithfully.

# Chapter 12
# College Life and Activities

Rockwood College is located on the northern edge of the city of Rockwood, Illinois on Lincoln Drive, across the street from the new Natural Museum. Rockwood College is 122 years old and boasts an enrollment of 1,271 students. There are 342 students accurately employed within the city and outlying communities. Many local residents patronize the college by their attendance at their sports games, plays and educational programs. There has always been a good relationship between Rockwood College and the city of Rockwood.

Rockwood College has a variety of interesting classes and activities to lure the young and especially the old back to school, the college they didn't have a chance to go to or couldn't afford because the were strapped financially.

Our tour guide gave us this account of the tour, "Upon entrance to the College from the south, we encounter a small non-denominational Chapel with church services every morning before classes start, with a good attendance, almost always, over crowded.

On any given morning many students can be seen walking to their classes at 8:00AM for their 1st class of the day, a fifty minute lecture, demonstration, and review whatever pertains to the subject they are studying. Students can be seen milling around all day long between classes at their lockers and then on to their next class. Some students join each other for the same class, while others wander off solo in search of that unique class only Rockwood College offers.

Off and on, all day long students can be seen entering Wellon's Dining Hall for a quick lunch, nothing elaborate, just filling, to tide them over to the next class within the hour.

As we meander down the hall, we reach Krier Auditorium with a beautiful stage and setting and exquisite seating capacity. Very accommodating, with a play in progress. In attendance are the fifth and sixth graders from Rockwood, Brown, and Morgan grade schools, all from the city of Rockwood. We sat down for a few minutes to watch the play which was called, "A Believers Trust."

After we watched several little settings we proceeded down the hall to other areas of interest.

We came upon the Music Room of the Rockwood College Band and stepped inside to a wide array of instruments in action to the tune of "God Bless America."

The music instructor saw us and introduced us to the band and we smiled and waved back and they did the same. We were careful not to disturb them from their practice.

As we left the music room we headed down the hall into several laboratory classes in action, dissecting for the day. Other classes too numerous to mention were enroute through out the college.

We also went into the weight lifting room and the indoor swimming area where students were swimming. An adjoining room was the bowling alley, with students at play, as we stepped inside for a few minutes to watch them bowl.

As we headed down the hallway we came upon the Rockwood College Gymnasium where some important sports games are played. We stood in the doorway and watched them practice for the next day's game and talked to some of the players for that game against their opponents Bixby College.

The next night's game, Rockwood vs. Bixby, brought a large crowd, as rival schools will do. The game starts at 7:00 PM with buses of people being chauffeured in advance from nearby communities. It is the main game of the basketball season. Rich Burns and his wife Lila, Carl Biller and his wife Pearl, Marcus Reil, and Sue Benson and her mother, Jane, are also going to the game in the Senior Citizens Bus, which has started taking senior citizens to games, plays and different outings in the daytime and evenings.

It is almost time for the game to start as the band has started playing its last tune. The tenants from the Rockwood Apartment Complex are all seated together in the bleachers cheering for Rockwood College. The game has just started and Rockwood is in the lead by two points. As the game progresses Rockwood is still in the lead 42-20 as the spectators continue to cheer the players on. It is now approaching half time as the players leave the court and everything settles down.

BANG! All of a sudden there is a loud, crackling noise coming out of the loudspeaker that startled everybody. The principal, Mr. Slavic, apologized for the noise and said, "I have an announcement to make and could I have everybody's attention because it is very important."

Mr. Slovic said, "There has been a bomb threat to Rockwood College called in about fifteen minutes ago. Please don't panic because we want everybody to evacuate the building in an orderly fashion, meaning single file. The game has been cancelled, to be resumed at a later date, or you can ask for your money back. I would rather everyone go on home, instead of standing around outside the college to see what happens. When you arrive home, turn your televisions on for the 10:00 PM news and there should be a report on there. Thank you."

The tenants called the Senior Citizen Bus and Marcus went on home with his car. When they arrived at the apartment complex they all gathered in the recreation parlor and turned on the television but it was still too early, so they watched a game show instead. When that was over they watched the 10:00 PM news. The announcer said, "Rockwood College received a bomb threat around 8:00 PM and the Bomb Squad was called in but nothing was found. A hoax? I'm sure! The police department is investigating who called in the bomb threat."

Several days have passed during the investigation and the results were about as expected. Three boys ages 18, 16 and 19, decided to call in a bomb threat at the height of the basketball season when there

*BLOOD SUCKING SERIES NO. 1: THE FINAL FLOOR*

would be a large crowd at a game, like the Rockwood vs. Bixby game. They enjoyed watching the crowd leave in a hurry, nervous and scared. They got a big kick out of that.

The police traced the bomb threat telephone call to the nineteen year olds house and immediately handcuffed them and booked them into jail to await trial at a later date.

One Month Later...

Barry Jones, Mark White, and Cliff Arnold went to trial for the telephone bomb threat made to a Rockwood College vs. Bixby College basketball game a month ago, March 3, 2000. The judge sentenced each of them to two years in prison, without parole.

The Rockwood College game vs. Bixby College will be played this Friday at 7:00PM in the Rockwood College Gymnasium. The Senior Citizen's Bus will take the apartment tenants to the game and back to the apartment complex again. Rich and his wife Lila, Carl Biller and his wife Pearl, Marcus Reil, and Sue Benson and her mother Jane are going to go back to watch them this coming Friday night at 7:00 PM at the Rockwood College Gymnasium. Marcus will also drive his car to the game, along with several other friends.

Rich Burns and Carl Biller are thinking seriously about taking computer classes at Rockwood College.

Rich and Carl both signed up for two months of computer and internet classes during the daytime hours. Rich bought himself a computer and internet, but Carl still has to get one. They started going to the classes Monday and Thursday at 2:00 PM. There are ten people to a class. They are being held at the Rockwood Senior Center free of charge. Everybody is welcome to join a class and new classes start every month.

Marcus bought himself an internet and computer and has decided to take classes also. He would like to learn how to e-mail to his mother and relatives in St. Louis, Missouri. Marcus would also like to e-mail to Betty in prison if she has access to a computer.

Sue and her mother Jane would also like to take the classes for the computer and internet training because neither of them understands how to operate it.

There are many different features at Rockwood College that students can take advantage of. For those that don't have access to a kitchen, don't like to cook or aren't experienced in the culinary arts they can participate in Dollar Night on Sunday evenings at 5:30 PM in the college dining room. It also defrays the expense of a meal otherwise. This is reserved for students only, so the local city people cannot apply themselves to this program. During the summer, when students are not at the college "Dollar Night" is closed until college resumes in the fall.

Parents of students that attend college here are on a working schedule to donate their time and talent to prepare wholesome, nutritious lunches and a clean up crew afterward. About three hundred and fifty students regularly attend "Dollar Night" from 5:30 PM until about 8:30 PM on Sunday nights only. Sometimes student's help in the clean up after all the lunches have been served if not enough parents are available.

Last Sunday night's menu consisted of cheeseburgers, French fries, a salad and a soft drink and brownies for dessert. The students have a choice of sitting at the dining room table or sacking their food and taking it to their residence. About half of the students eat in the dining room and the other half take it to their residence. "Dollar Night" has grown in popularity among the students and over the years has saved them a considerable amount of money on their meals. The students are very appreciative of this program and look forward to their Sunday night lunch and fellowship with other students.

On Sunday nights in winter different soups and dinner rolls are brought in for the students to partake of, plus a variety of desserts consisting of cake, brownies, ice cream, cookies, etc.

Many students are saying that they are currently employed on the college grounds, inside and out, in maintenance and cleaning and otherwise. Some students are employed in the city of Rockwood itself, plus those that are working in the out lying communities of Bixby and Plattsville. They commute back and forth to Rockwood and car pool with friends that have similar situations. It helps to defray the cost of the fuel. Most students are working, others are there on scholarships and some are lucky enough to come from wealthy families where money isn't a problem for the college student. Other students are going to school on a loan, that is borrowing money to go to school and paying it back once they are out of college and have the funds to pay their loan back. Everybody's monetary situation is different for college.

Another activity Rockwood College provides in the summer is their weekly band concert in the band shell in Lincoln Park, south of Rockwood College. It is free and open to the public. In case of rain it is transferred to the college auditorium. It begins every Thursday at 8:00 PM and is over at 10:00 PM. Sometimes they have live singers, local and out of town musicians to perk up the entertainment. They are always represented with a large crowd of people, bringing their lawn chairs and picnic coolers and some sitting on the bleachers. Once in awhile the ice cream wagon or a sandwich van stops and they will be patronized.

Rockwood College also offers a wide variety of plays open to the public every Tuesday night at 8:00 PM (in the summer only) at Krier auditorium. They have a minimum charge of five dollars per couple or three dollars for one person only. They have a schedule of plays posted in the local newspaper, The Rockwood Flyer" among the other summer activities at the college and within the city of Rockwood.

Rich Burns Lila, Carl Biller and his wife Pearl, Sue Benson and her mother, Jane, are going to have the Senior Citizen Bus pick them up to go to the play this evening at the Krier Auditorium at the college at 8:00 PM. They have to start coming earlier because the attendance is seating capacity only and standing room is not allowed. Marcus Reil picked up a few friends and they are planning on attending the play weather permitting. When Marcus and his friends pulled up to the college, the radio announcer was broadcasting a severe thunderstorm headed for Rockwood, Illinois with winds up to 90 miles an hour and baseball sized hail in the city of Rockwood and the surrounding area. A tornado has been sighted about fifty miles west of Rockwood, Illinois.

Nothing has been broadcast about taking precautions and seeking a sturdy shelter in your home.

People are filing into the west entrance of the Krier Auditorium to take their seats for the play. As they were getting seated, a sudden clap of thunder made everyone jump and exclaim, as a streak of lightening zig zagged through the windows, like fingers of light grasping the sky.

A few people got up to depart, while others shuddered and began to panic. Suddenly, the curtain rose and the cast of characters in the play made their appearance amidst a thunder of applause. The title of the play is "Pennies from Heaven," a highly acclaimed presentation from anyone who witnessed the play. Periodically, throughout the play, there were claps of thunder and zig zag lightening and an outpouring of rain. As everybody was gazing at the stage, a sharp crack of thunder and lightening split the roof above the stage and rain came pouring in on the cast of characters and audience drenching them like drowned rats. Part of the roof crashed onto the stage, the cast of characters and the audience. Boards and shingles fell on everybody's heads amidst screams and cries for help. Victims were sitting in their seats dazed and overcome with the impact of it all, everything was too much to comprehend because it all happened in a flash. Rich, Lila, Pearl and Sue were drastically injured as they all had large, open gashes on their head with a steady stream of blood flowing out and everybody had numerous cuts and bruises on their bodies, plus torn skin. Nobody was left unscathed, because everyone felt some sort of impact on their body when the roof collapsed.

The police department, ambulance and paramedics arrived upon the scene within minutes of getting a call from the college. The ambulance wheeled in several gurney's to transport victims back to Rockwood Hospital with life threatening injuries. Rich, Lila, Pearl and Sue were taken to the hospital by Marcus. The emergency room and waiting rooms were full of victims with deep cuts, similar to those of the Rockwood Apartment Complex tenants. Several older people were injured severely and didn't recover, thus passing away in the ambulance on the way to Rockwood hospital. Luckily, not more people from the Rockwood Apartment Complex attended the play or their would've been more gashes and injuries.

Marcus waited till everyone had been treated at the emergency room and then he delivered everyone to their apartment. At this point, a light rain was still coming down, but the wind had subsided. The announcer on the radio reported a tornado had gone through the area of Lincoln Street, where the school is situated. Several other homes in the area had their roofs torn off and gaping holes in the sides of their houses. Three people have died because of the velocity of the tornado."

# Chapter 13
# Police Chief's Mother Murdered

Mrs. Jean Blane is an 81 year old retired widow mother of the Police Chief Charles Blane of the Rockwood Police Department that moved into the Rockwood Apartment Complex six weeks ago from her home on the east end of the city. Her husband, Dick, passed away three years ago of a sudden heart attack. He was an attorney with Blane, Blare and Burton Attorneys and Jean was the secretary at the office. Her other son, Nick, is an Attorney in New York City. Her finances allowed her to move into the apartments and eliminate a maid and a groundskeeper much to her advantage.

Jean takes the elevator on Tuesday nights to the main lobby, and then she joins the others in the recreation parlor for some games of pinochle. Rich, his wife Lila, Carl, Sue, Marcus and herself play pinochle till about 10:00 PM, not for money, just for fun. After the pinochle games Jean takes the elevator back up to her apartment, where she retires for the evening.

One night, someone knocked at her door and Jean answered, "Oh, come in Charles, how good to see you. I haven't seen you since we went out for lunch over a week ago. How have you, Jan and the kids been doing? I've been meaning to call."

"I just got off work at the Police Department and I knew you'd still be up. I thought I'd drop by on my way home and see if you needed anything from the grocery store or otherwise," said Charles.

"That's sweet of you, Charles, but I really don't need anything. I just got back upstairs from playing pinochle with my friends in the recreation parlor. Our team lost. I guess I didn't get the right cards. We always have a snack while we play pinochle. Tonight we had ice tea and Lila baked some peanut butter cookies for us. I brought a few upstairs. Let me get you one to sample." Jean handed Charles a cookie and he ate it and said, "That's delicious, Mom. Ask her for the recipe so you can bake a couple of dozen for me. That's my favorite cookie since I was a kid, remember?"

"Yes, I remember that Charles and I will ask her tomorrow because I'll be playing bridge with her in the afternoon."

Charles asked his mother how things were doing at the apartment complex and she said, "Fine, no problems." He said, "Well, I guess I have to go now because Jan and the kids are waiting up for me. I want to get home before it starts to rain."

Jean said, "Just a minute Charles, how are the repairs coming along at the college after the tornado? I haven't been by there since you and I drove by early last week before lunch."

"There making progress and it's beginning to look improved. It'll take awhile till everything gets back to normal. That was a bad deal. Very devastating. Guess I'll be going now, Mom. Call me if you need anything. Okay? Goodnight."

Jean said, "Okay, Charles, Goodnight." She then retired for the evening.

A notice was posted on the bulletin board of the apartment complex that Ladies Bridge Club would be playing their weekly bridge game in the recreation parlor. There will be two tables of bridge with six ladies to a table. The games start at two o'clock. Jean Blane is hurriedly getting ready in her apartment because she intends to pick her partner for the bridge game and so do other ladies. Most of the ladies get downstairs to the recreation parlor earlier for that reason.

Jean left her apartment at 1:45 PM, locked the door and headed for the elevator with her walking cane. The elevators at the apartment complex have two sides to them, so Jean entered one side and was getting ready to push the down button when she sensed something other than herself in the elevator. She immediately turned around and was confronted by a large, enraged snarling pit bull dog. Both elevator doors were closed and wouldn't re-open. That's strange. Was it a possible malfunction of the doors? What's happening?

Who let the pit bull into the elevator? Jean hadn't seen anything. At this point the pit bull is edging closer, while Jean is pushing against the back wall of the elevator more. Jean is petrified with fear, crying and screaming.

"Help me, help me someone! There's a pit bull in the elevator and I'm scared! Please get some help," but no one answered because all the ladies were at the bridge game. "He's going to attack me. Please get some help," Jean continued to scream. Still no answer. By this time, the pit bull was about two feet away from Jean with his mouth gaping wide open and his eyes sparked with red, hot rage as his growl became deeper and more meaningful. The pit bull got extremely agitated as Jean continued to scream, cry and beg for help.

In a mere second, catching Jean off guard, the pit bull lunged at Jean, as she crashes to the floor, in a wild attempt to balance her frail and weakened ninety five pound frame. As she tries to recover from her fall, the pit bull pounces on her chest and bites Jean on the cheek, leaving a huge gaping hole in her face, the size of a silver dollar with blood gushing out uncontrollably, with her skin sticking between the pit bull's teeth. He continued mauling her face, biting her eye out of the socket and spitting it on the floor. By now she has quit screaming, her body motionless, semi-unconscious and close to death, as the pit bull is still on his rampage.

As Jean is lying on the elevator floor, the pit bull mauled her head, tearing hunks of hair out of her scalp and trying to chew them between his large teeth. Low moans and gurgling sounds keep escaping out of Jean's throat, as her eyes open and close in death. A glazed look covers the one eye as it protrudes from its socket. The elevator doors are still closed as the pit bull stands over Jean panting for air and glaring and barking at her.

He makes another attempt to jump on her chest and bite her in the jugular vein in her neck causing blood to run without stopping. A huge pool of blood had collected on the floor and streaks of blood were all over the walls and even on the ceiling. Body parts scattered over the floor. Jean lay in death in a heap on the floor while the pit bull glared at her and continued to bark. In the meantime, the killer slipped in and put a note in her hand saying, "This is not the last death."

All of a sudden, the elevator gives a jerk and the one door opens and the pit bull dashed out of the elevator leaving Jean dead. Carl passes by and just happens to glance toward the elevator and lets out a yell. "Help somebody, call an ambulance, please. There's been a mauling and death in the elevator. Hurry!"

Now, at this time of the afternoon the bridge players are concluding their game and some of the ladies are ready to get on the elevator to go back to their apartments. Because of everything that had transpired they had to take the back stairs. Everybody was shocked and stricken with grief at what had happened. The police, ambulance, paramedics and dog catcher are already on the scene of the deadly mauling of Jean Blane by an unidentifiable pit bull which was in the area. The dog catcher has already left the scene in search of the pit bull while the police are questioning, interviewing and investigating and fingerprinting the case. The ambulance has picked up Jean's mangled and dismembered body and transported it to Rockwood Hospital for confirmation of death and then on to Brown Mortuary for the final preparations.

Charles and his family were notified immediately and overcome with grief as Charles said, "I just went to see Mom last night after I got off work at the police department and she was fine. She commented on the delicious peanut butter cookies Rich's wife, Lila, had baked and I told her jokingly to get the recipe, so she could make a couple of dozen for me. She gave me a cookie to sample and I told her they were very good. She was planning on getting the recipe and baking some for me. I guess I won't get them anymore now."

Charles brother, Nick from New York City arrived with his family today flabbergasted at the type of death his mother had to endure, from a pit bull dog.

Jean's casket was closed at the Brown Mortuary because she was a victim of unusual circumstances, which did not allow them to open the casket for viewing. Dozens of mourners filed in for the final service and burial at Rockwood Cemetery in the next several days. Everyone was invited to a luncheon in the church basement, which was well attended.

## The Search Goes On...

After Charles, Nick and their families endured the mourning period, Nick and his family is in New York City again and life has hopefully gotten back to normal for Charles and his family again.

The city dog catcher also remarked, "We searched for the pit bull and found him wandering around in the park the next day with no identification or any other way to trace him to his owner. At present he is at the dog pound awaiting identification."

The Rockwood Police Department is aware that all of these deaths at the Rockwood Apartment Complex are attributed to the work of one person or persons because of the note that was clutched in Jean's hand stating, "This is not the last death." The police said, "We have taken the note and tried to analyze it, basically matching it up with known suspects, ex-criminals, or people that have just been booked into jail in the last day or two. No luck so far."

Detectives Blount and Still are back in Illinois from St. Louis, Missouri to assist in the investigation of the pit bull death of Jean Blane. Early Monday morning Detective Blount and Still are on there way to Bixby and Plattsville, Illinois to visit the dog pounds of different communities in reference to the death of Jean Blane. So far they haven't come up with anything. On the way back they stopped at a town called Simpsonville for a little information about their community and dog pound. The pit bull that mauled and bit Jean is hard to trace because he has no identification on him, and very few people in town have pit bulls. "Where did he come from? Who brought him into the apartment complex?" Jean had a note clutched in her hand when they found her on the floor. "Where did the note come from?"

Not knowing where else to turn for help Charles, the Chief of Police, decided to take a different approach in this investigation of his mother's death. Since no one knows where the pit bull came from, no identification tag and no information on him, Charles decided to put an APB (All Points Bulletin) out on the pit bull itself, although everybody knows he's at the dog pound.

Charles explained to the policeman at the meeting that, "The All Points Bulletin on the pit bull is being used to bring the owner of the pit bull forward, acknowledging that he owns the dog, and why he is running around without a tag. After he owns up to the ownership of the dog, then we need to see if he is somehow involved in the death of my mother."

I want these "All Points Bulletins" posted in the store windows, cafés, and service stations, anywhere people can see them. Even on the lamp posts and poles on the corners. If this is your pit bull, please come forward and claim your dog, as we have him in custody. Our phone number is 501-234-4424. Please call."

"Please circulate these flyers (All Points Bulletin) all over town. Thank you!"

Not long after flyers were distributed an oriental man came forward to claim the pit bull. The oriental man explained the pit bull ran away or got stolen out in the country where he lives. The police brought him down to the police station to be on display in case someone decides to claim him for their own. When the oriental man entered the police station, he said he would recognize his dog by certain markings. Well, the markings weren't there and the pit bull got upset all of a sudden and almost bit the oriental man in the hand. The oriental man got very angry at the police, swore under his breath and stomped out of the room.

Charles decided to take the "All Points Bulletin" Friday and post it to the pit bull's cage and also on the internet hoping someone will respond. "I would like to see my wishes fulfilled, that someone will come forward and claim this pit bull and also possibly have a hand in the death of my mother for my mother's sake, so justice will be served," as he wiped the tears from his eyes once again.

Charles made the comment, "We will also announce it on the radio and present a flyer on television and our telephone number and see what happens."

Several weeks passed and nothing happened. A few more people stopped by the police station to look at the pit bull, but it wasn't their dog. Charles said, "Maybe the owner doesn't want to claim the pit bull for fear of being tied in with my mother's death. Get it?" Several policemen said, "That's a very strong possibility, Chief."

One day Charles, the police chief, made the remark while he was having his usual morning cup of coffee to several of the policemen in his office, "Well, it's been over a month since my mother was mauled to death by that damn bastard of a dog. Actually, I won't do this, but, I feel like shooting that ugly devil myself. This has been a hard tribulation for our family to cope with. I hope and pray that no one else has to experience what we are going through."

One of the policemen spoke for the other two saying, "Chief, we realize what you and your family are going through and we offer our condolences hoping this case is solved and justice is served."

Charles wiped some tears from his eyes again and said, "Thank you, men. I appreciate that because I know you care a lot." I hope we get some answers soon. The officers agreed and left the office, leaving Charles with his thoughts.

To make matters worse, while Charles was engrossed in his thoughts, the phone rang and he answered, "Rockwood Police Department, may I help you?"

A young boy on the line with several others in the background said laughingly, "We know who owns the pit bull! We know who owns the pit bull! Wouldn't you like to know?" CLICK! They hung up and Charles was madder than ever, determined to find out who they were by tracing the phone call. After completing the tracing Charles sent one of his policemen, Officer Lee, out to a certain address to take care of the problem and bring them in to the police station. When he arrived

## BLOOD SUCKING SERIES NO. 1: THE FINAL FLOOR

Officer Lee could see them through the window locking the door, but he still knocked on the door and identified himself. When they didn't open he kicked in the front door and proceeded into the house. He found three boys, ages 9, 10 and 12 years old, huddled in a closet, afraid of being found. Officer Lee coaxed them out of the closet and told them he would have to fill out a report and take all three of them to the juvenile section of the police department for further questioning, because of the nature of the call in which the police chief's mother was mauled to death.

A trial date was set for August 7, 2000 and Bobby Jones, Joe Mullen and Jack Shill were brought to court in a short hearing, the judge sentencing them to serve one month in juvenile detention in spite of school starting.

Their parents were in agreement with the sentencing saying, "This will teach them a lesson. They will think twice about doing something like that again, no telephone privileges, and they are grounded."

The Rockwood Police Department is no closer to solving the mauling death of Jean Blane, than the day it happened, almost two months ago. The pit bull continues to be in custody at the police department until further investigation warrants him being taken back to the pound. The pit bull doesn't answer to any pet name, no identification, no registration anywhere, no leads and no clues. Nothing! Seems strange, doesn't it?

The surrounding towns around Rockwood have been checked also, for stray pit bulls and there aren't any, because a pit bull is a rare breed of dog and there aren't that many around. The pit bull that mauled Jean Blane to death has an owner, but they aren't coming forward for fear of getting caught and going to prison for life.

Let's see what happens down the road.

# CHAPTER 14
# A NEW DEPUTY

Marcus Reil is beginning to re-surface in the whole gruesome picture of the Rockwood Apartment Complex murders. Marcus still works faithfully every day as a janitor at the Rockwood College. He now has an apartment and a second hand car to get around in. His girlfriend, Betty, is in prison for two years in Plattsville, Illinois with no chance for parole. Betty seriously harassed a couple of ladies she worked for as a maid and was reported and apprehended. Marcus has made a few friends in the city, but his acquaintances are limited. He still plays Pinochle on Wednesday nights at the Rockwood Apartments with Rich, Carl and the others.

Before playing Pinochle one night Marcus happened to pick up the local newspaper, The Rockwood Flyer, and thumb through it, not looking for anything in particular. A quick look at the "Wanted Ads" wouldn't interest him, or so he thought until he came upon the "Wanted Ads" by the Rockwood Police Department, looking for a deputy, to fill in when Charles and his family were out of town. Marcus thought, "What did he know about being a deputy? I'm sure they would probably train him if a trained deputy didn't apply for the job. It was worth a try. He would apply after he got off work Monday afternoon, which he did. Charles told him, "We've had the ad in the paper about six weeks already and no one has applied, so he said he would hire Marcus and give him on the job training, target practice, detective work and everything that pertains to the job of a deputy.

Marcus reported for his janitorial job at 7:00 AM in the morning and worked until 3:00 PM in the afternoon and then went on to his training as one of the deputies for Jean Blane's murder. His training consists of target practice everyday, the different phases of local detective work within the city, accompanying a trained detective to different murder scenes for first hand information, they need to work with etc... After his initial training is completed Marcus is then assigned to a beat with another deputy or policeman on the evening shift, patrolling the streets of Rockwood.

Sunday, Marcus and several other men will be deputized in a small informal ceremony at the police station open to the public at 2:00 PM. Marcus and the other men are all excited. Marcus wishes Betty, his girlfriend, was present to witness this ceremony. After the ceremony, Marcus will place a call to Betty to tell her all about it, because he knows she will be elated.

The next night he was on his first beat with another policeman, Ben, to patrol the alleys and side streets for anything unusual or out of place.

As they cruised through the alleys they encountered several young boys, about 12 years of age, smoking cigarettes beside a building. Ben stopped the patrol car and Marcus walked over to them and said, "You boys better get out of this dark alley and throw those cigarettes away because your to young to smoke. You never know who your liable to encounter in these dark, deserted areas. C'mon, lets move on." The boys took his advice and Ben and Marcus drove on. At 11:00 PM the midnight shift comes on, so Ben and Marcus drove back to the police station to go home. "Nothing exciting going on tonight," said Marcus. "Everything's as dead as a doornail. I figured it would be because there aren't any baseball games in town tonight. That accounts for a lot." Ben said, "I know," as they proceeded on home.

Charles and his family are leaving town on business for a week, which puts newly deputized Marcus in total charge of Jean Blane's murder case for the time being. Marcus studies the current investigative reports on the murder case, especially the fingerprint file to see if anything different has been added, since the case started. Everything is basically the same, but Marcus might look for a few twists or turns, if possible. He went to the Rockwood Apartment Complex around suppertime to check the elevator again and interview several more people living there.

Carl Biller and his wife, Pearl, had just finished eating supper when Marcus knocked on the door and was immediately led in by Pearl. Marcus said, "Sorry for intruding, but I just decided to ask you a few more questions, and take a closer look at all the evidence we have and go from there.

After the interview Marcus thanked Carl and Pearl for their time and hoped he didn't take up too much of it. Carl said in reply, Sorry, we couldn't be of more help." He left their 4$^{th}$ floor apartment and headed for the elevator to see if anything was left undetected. The elevator walls and ceiling had been scrubbed down and re-painted, a new carpet was installed, and all evidence was accounted for. Any trace of anything that was noteworthy was missing. Marcus left the apartment building rather disappointed, because there were no facts or evidence to base anything on. As he headed back to the police station, he decided to check out another issue concerning Jean Blane's murder case, namely fingerprints. That is fingerprints, regarding the pit bull, which is in custody at the police station. Marcus went outside into the police yard, west of the police station, and walked over to the fenced in area with a screened in top housing the pit bull. He is pacing back and forth, apparently agitated, and snarling and baring his teeth as Marcus approaches him. Marcus said a few words and the pit bull continues to snarl and jump onto the fence. Marcus repeated, "What's the matter, you mean, ugly, old pit bull? Cat got your tongue? I hate your guts. I wish someone would shoot you. I'd like to, but I daren't. I should be so lucky. You, devil, you! Hah!" Marcus kept staring at the pit bull for some uncanny reason, he doesn't know why. He is looking at his hair, facial features, ears and body structure. His eyes drop to his paws, with their clean, cut, padding of skin underneath. Could it be possible? No, surely not! But, how does he really know, except to ask another fellow policeman or deputy. In the recesses of his mind,

## BLOOD SUCKING SERIES NO. 1: THE FINAL FLOOR

Marcus pictures a person, possibly positioning a pit bull's paws while in the elevator, telling him to stay in that position. Also, the note is in the possession of the police department. Charles, the Chief of Police said, "We didn't find any fingerprints on the note, so whoever put the note in Jean's hand wore gloves, as simple as that.

Marcus is still not satisfied in regards to the pit bulls paws. He is asking himself, "Could the killer have their fingerprints on the pit bulls paws? Why not? Has anybody ever fingerprinted the pit bulls paws? Might be a good idea." Marcus said, "I'm going to leave that for tomorrow." About this time, Marcus got in his car for the drive home.

The next evening as Marcus was on his way to the police station, he vowed he would take the fingerprints of the pit bulls paws. As he walked toward the pit bull and gently coaxed him out of his pen, the pit bull came up to the fence and acted as if he knew him from somewhere else. Marcus let himself into the pen as the pit bull came forward, picked up every paw and stamped it on a fingerprinting pad, and then onto a piece of paper for the imprint. Marcus was trying to get a human fingerprint from under the paws of the pit bull. Marcus was told by another policeman, "The pit bulls paws have never been fingerprinted before." After they fingerprinted the pit bulls paws they compared them with inmates of the jail, unsavory characters spending several nights in jail, and people with a suspicious nature. Everyone's imprint proved negative, so Marcus was convinced of that.

Since Marcus is in charge of Jean Blane's murder investigation at the present moment, he decided to fingerprint the tenants at the Rockwood Apartment Complex because that's where all the murders have been taking place.

The next afternoon Marcus drove to the Rockwood Apartment Complex and fingerprinted all of the tenants, except several that weren't there, namely Carl and Pearl Biller and Jane Linton, Sue's mother because they were all out of town. Marcus said, "Oh, that's okay if there not here, I'm sure there okay."

The results were very pleasing to Marcus and the tenants of the Rockwood Apartment Complex, because they were all negative.

When Charles, the police chief, and his family, came back from their business trip Marcus explained the pit bull paws of fingerprinting and also the tenants at the Rockwood Apartment Complex. Charles was amazed and said, "Very well done, Marcus. I'm proud of you. I knew I could leave you in charge. In fact I also have an idea to contribute to that. I'm thinking about putting an article in our local paper, "The Rockwood Flyer," in regards to everybody in Rockwood coming to some building, which I haven't established yet, to get themselves fingerprinted. If they don't show up they will have a fine enforced on them. We will start out with the letter "A". Anybody in town with a last name that begins with A will have so much time to come in and get fingerprinted. The police have a list of all the last names in town and they are alphabetized, so if someone doesn't show up they are aware of it. After that it will be the B's and on down the alphabet, until the whole alphabet is accounted for. We might be surprised what turns up. I'll get to work on it right away tomorrow morning, securing a building and whatever's involved."

The next morning Charles secured the local 4-H building for the fingerprinting job which will start in three days and it will be manned by policemen from the police force in the city. The Arts Building at Rockwood College will be reserved for the fingerprinting process to eliminate confusion at the 4-H Building in town. So far everybody is conforming to the standards of the police's request for everybody in Rockwood to be fingerprinted from 21 years of age on up. A few people ignored the request and were issued a hefty fine.

Weeks Later...

By now half of the city has been fingerprinted with the other half still to go. So far everything has been negative. Several people had to be fingerprinted a couple of times because it showed up suspicious and positive, but then finally turned out negative. What a neat way to reverse the worry, from the community of Rockwood, to a lighter note.

## BLOOD SUCKING SERIES NO. 1: THE FINAL FLOOR

Time passes on as all people 21 years of age have been fingerprinted within the city of Rockwood and at the college with negative results.

And as Marcus was saying, "Thank God for that, but still somehow, someway, somewhere there is someone with the fingerprints the police are looking for. I'm positive of that." We're just going to have to look longer and farther. And we're going to need help from a higher authority, namely God. Marcus' shift ended an hour earlier tonight, so on the way home he stopped at a nondenominational church on the way to and from work, for some prayers and reflection. Marcus implored, "God, please help us in apprehending the killer and put an end to the killings at the Rockwood Apartment Complex." After much prayerful thoughts Marcus said, "Lord, they will be done. Amen." Marcus left the church and drove home to eat supper, read the newspaper and watch television. He retired about 10:00 PM as usual.

About 3:00 AM the phone rang and startled Marcus out of a sound sleep, as he nearly jumped out of bed. Officer Lee was on the other end of the line saying, "Marcus, sorry to disturb your sleep, but can you come down to the police station right away? It's in the line of duty. The pit bull that we're harboring has been released and possibly stolen. Come immediately."

Marcus quickly got dressed and left with a light rain falling. The streets were deserted, yet an occasional car would go by, as he neared the police station. Marcus got out of his car and went to the west end of the building where several policemen and Charles, the police chief, were congregated. The gate had been broken into with a wrench or pliers and the pit bull was coaxed out of the fence. Footprints of the pit bull and another person, it could be either a man or a woman footprint, can be seen on the yard inside the fence. Charles told the men, "We'll wait until morning and call the animal shelter and have the dog catcher go out and see if he can be found. The policemen came back here periodically to check on him, because I was working late on my papers and I saw them. So, in between checks, someone came, broke the lock and released him. What a mess we're in again, now with the actual evidence stolen. Dammit! I wonder who in the Sam hell is behind all these killings. Once we catch them, I swear, they'll be in prison for life, if I have anything to do with it. What do you men think of this? He asked his policemen. The policemen whole heartedly said, "We all agree, Chief, because now our main evidence has been stolen and we have nothing to go on. What on earth are we going to do, Chief?' Charles answered, "I don't know. Something has to be figured out pretty damn soon. These killings can't go on like this. Something's got to be done. Anybody have any suggestions?" We'll listen to anything.

Marcus suggested, "Chief, if we got the pit bull back again, we might have one of several options, such as placing him back in the animal shelter where he was at first, bringing him inside the police station permanently or if he is going to live outside in his pen, some policemen will have to take shifts guarding him, so this doesn't happen again. You see what havoc this creates?"

"Well said, Marcus, you have some good points there," said Charles.

Two Weeks Later...

Two weeks have passed since the pit bull was stolen and still no sign of him. The dog catcher has been out everyday looking for the pit bull, but to no avail, he's nowhere to be found. Finally, one day, several policemen and a detective were investigating something at Thunder Creek when Officer Lee yelled, "Look over there! That looks like a pit bull. Sure enough, it is. That's the one we're looking for. Let's call the dog catcher!" An officer instantly called the city dog catcher and he was on his way. He was there in twenty minutes, caught the pit bull and went back to the animal shelter with him. They put him in a secluded area, inside away from the other animals, so that there would be minimum distraction.

The Rockwood Animal shelter has explicit instructions not to give away or sell the pit bull because he is being confined as strong evidence in the mauling death of Jean Blane. And he's not open to public viewing at the animal shelter, because of his notoriety in the death of Jean Blane.

*BLOOD SUCKING SERIES NO. 1: THE FINAL FLOOR*

## August 2000

The evenings are getting just a little longer in spite of the last days of summer according to the calendar.

On Marcus' day off, which falls on a Wednesday sometimes, he still plays cards on that night with the Pinochle group consisting of Carl and Pearl Biller, Rich Burns and Lila and Sue Benson and her mother Jane Linton in the recreation parlor at 7:00 PM. A table of snacks always accompanies the card players wherever they maybe.

Not too soon after the conversation started, it immediately drifted into the recent, grisly murder of Jean Blane and the pit bull. Everybody asked a deluge of questions, including Sue's mother Jane, a demure, quiet, soft spoken woman who rarely ever raises her voice to join in the conversation.

Marcus, since he's been deputized, is limited on the information he can disclose, but he did tell them the pit bull has been located and is being kept in an undisclosed location, so there won't be a repetition of his disappearance again. Other questions that were relevant to the issue were asked, which Marcus answered as best he could without divulging too much information. Jane asked Marcus a question or two about the pit bull murder, with no important significants.

All of a sudden Sue asked her mother Jane, "Mother, I completely forgot to ask you this. Don't tell me you were out taking a walk the night Jean Blane was mauled by that pit bull? Because I distinctly remember you were gone. Do you know how dangerous that was with that enraged pit bull on the loose and you out there walking? I told you not to be out walking at night by yourself without me or someone else along." Jane said, "Oh, Sue, you worry too much. I went to bed extra early and couldn't sleep, so I got dressed and decided to take a walk for awhile. In fact, I walked downtown and did a little shopping and stopped in at Casey's Restaurant for a sandwich and coffee. Remember, I showed you that blue top I bought at Markley's Department Store? I remember when I got back they said the pit bull had run off and the police, detectives, ambulance and paramedics were still here. I inquired what had happened and they told me. I was so shocked because I knew

Jean Blane very well. In fact, we used to play bridge together on the same team. I really miss her. We always had such a wonderful time. I'll never forget her." Everyone was sitting and listening intently, while Jane was elaborating on her acquaintance with Jean Blane, since Jane doesn't speak up very often. Even Sue was surprised for a change.

A slow drizzle is beginning to form on the windows, a forecast for more rain to come, amidst a rise in the temperature for tomorrow.

The Pinochle game is drawing to a close with Marcus' team winning again. Everybody is saying their goodbyes, as Marcus said his day off next week is Wednesday, so he plans on coming back at 7:00 PM to participate in a Pinochle game again.

Everybody goes to the elevator to their respective apartments as Marcus leaves in a down pour by now, headed for home, a good, warm bath, and a little television. By then, he'll be ready to retire for the evening. Lying in bed and listening to the rain, Marcus goes over the days activities in his mind, the Pinochle game and the conversation—as he drifts off to sleep.

# Chapter 15
# Town Hall Meeting

Police chief, Charles Blane, is requesting a televised town hall meeting to be held tomorrow evening at 7:00 PM, weather permitting at the old Rockwood Town Hall on the south end of Main Street. He is encouraging some discussion on the murders and the evaluation of the pit bull case.

The weather is sunny and clear the next day, as the people file in to attend the meeting. The hall is overflowing as people are edging there way in and taking a seat wherever they can find one. Some latecomers will be standing against the wall for lack of room to sit down. The seating capacity of the hall is 200 people. Free coffee is available at a side table for anyone that would enjoy a cup.

All the tenants at the Rockwood Apartment Complex and Rockwood College are present this evening, plus tenants from other apartment complexes, local city people and the farming community. Police Chief, Charles, is conducting the meeting at the front table, with Marcus and several policemen joining him. Charles explains the nature of the meeting and is open to all discussions on various issues.

Rich stands up, identifies himself, where he lives and proceeds to pose the first question of the evening. Police Chief, "Have you given up on the first murder that occurred in 1995 of Fern Taylor, or are you just focused on the present murders?"

The Police Chief answered, "We are gathered here this evening to answer any and all questions that come to your mind. Please speak up if you want to address an issue. As for your question, Rich, Yes, we are still focused on all the murders that have taken place since Fern Taylor's murder in 1995. We believe that one and the same person is responsible for all of these murders, possibly excluding the young woman that was found in the tall weeds at Thunder Creek months ago. I hope that answers your question, Rich."

Rich nodded, and said, "Yes." The Police Chief asked again for questions from the assembly.

Sue stood up, identified herself as a resident of the Rockwood Apartment Complex and proceeded with her question: Police Chief, "Can you give us a detailed description of the pit bull murder of Jean Blane."

The Police Chief answered, "Yes, I believe I can, even though it was my own mother. The issue has to be brought up sooner or later for the benefit of all of us here this evening. As most of us are aware of, my mother came into the elevator to go downstairs to play bridge with some of her friends. When she stepped into the elevator, the pit bull pounced on her and mauled her repeatedly, until she was disfigured to the point of unrecognition. The pit bull raced out of the apartment complex and my mother was left dismembered and dead. The pit bull was caught by the next day and hauled to the animal shelter and then to the police station, where someone released him one night and he was gone for several weeks. One of our policemen recognized him and the dog catcher retrieved him again and took him back to the animal shelter where he is kept inside.

At this point, no one has come forward to claim the pit bull, nor has anybody's fingerprints matched those of the underside of the pit bulls paws, nor the note that was clutched in Jean Blane's hand the day of the murder. We're at a dead end. If anybody out there has any information or ideas to catch the killer or killers please come forward, as our family has a reward of $3,000.00 if your information leads to the apprehension of the killer or killers. If you're not sure of the information you have, please come forward anyway, because you never know. Stranger things have happened." I hope I have clarified this issue for you, Sue and thank you for asking." Sue smiled and said, "That was a sufficient answer, Police Chief"

The Police Chief asked, "Does anybody else have a question?" A lady in the last row raised her hand and answered, "My name is Joan Baker and I live in the Evans Apartment up the street, I have a question. Have you still not been able to release the name of the young woman found in the weeds at Thunder Creek?"

The Police Chief answered, "No, I'm sorry to say not and I'll tell you why. The young woman had no identification on her whatsoever, so we couldn't notify any next of kin. That's why she's buried in an unmarked grave at the cemetery. Yes, that was also a sad case."

"Anybody else have any question they want addressed? Now's the time to speak up," said the Police Chief again.

Dan Blyth sitting in the front row, stood up and said he had a question he'd like to have answered, and the Police Chief said, "Okay, we're going to try. What is it you want to know, Dan?"

Dan said, "I own Dan's Diner across the street from the Rockwood Apartment Complex and I'd like to know why all the killings that are occurring are always in the Rockwood Apartment Complex? It seems like that apartment complex has been singled out for all the murders. Why is that? Can anyone figure that out? I can't. For awhile, I was tempted to move my small restaurant business somewhere else. I was getting scared, since my restaurant is in close proximity to the apartments. I decided to stay because the rent is reasonable, business is brisk and it's too much work to move. The time when I'm scared is when I open up in the morning, and it's still dark and naturally in the evening when it's also dark. You just never know who can come walking through that front door.

The Police Chief commented, "I wish I could tell you, Dan, why they always strike at the Rockwood Apartment Complex, but I don't have a clear cut answer for that, and I don't think anybody else does either. Possibly, they think the people are an easy target in the elevator, because all the killings are happening in an elevator. Maybe, after they have done their evil deed, they have easier access to get away from the Rockwood Apartment Complex. And maybe they live close by, you never know. There can be a variety of reasons and maybe some we don't even think of." I wish I knew the answer."

The Police Chief said, "It's only nine o'clock. We have some time yet, so does anybody like to ask another question or make a comment, please stand up." A man sitting over to the side stood up and said, "My name is Bob Bean and I live a little way's down the street toward town and I'd like to make a comment about the residents of the Rockwood Apartment Complex. I've seen a group of them walking by towards the downtown area, like everybody knows where there from. It seems like their advertising it intentionally and when they go back home they get chased. I remember when that happened because I was sitting on my porch that night and it was announced over the radio. They should probably all go together in a taxi, come back in a taxi and split the fare. That way it would be safer for them. The person that chased them one night knows exactly where they live.

The Police Chief made the remark, "I agree with you, Bob, the residents of the Rockwood apartment Complex should be a little more discreet about their comings and goings. When they are all leaving the complex together, anybody that happens to see them knows exactly where they all live, and can follow them anytime they want. I agree, for awhile, it might be in their best interest to call a taxi and split the fare. It would be much safer."

The police Chief made the statement, "Everybody, let's take a coffee break for about fifteen minutes and then we'll resume the meeting, Okay?" Everybody nodded.

Fifteen Minutes Later…

The Police Chief said, "It's time to start the meeting again. Does anybody want to step forward with a question?" A young woman, in the middle of the hall raised her hand and said, "Good evening, my name is Shelly Crow and I attend Rockwood College. I just attended this meeting this evening to voice my opinion on all the problems at the apartment complex. Yes, I do think the residents at the apartment complex need to take a taxi together for the time being, till everything is resolved. They are just throwing caution to the wind and taking a chance, as they already have been followed a couple of times.

I also think they are striking here at the complex all the time because they allow transients to loiter in the lobby, watch television, and even spend the night which they cannot do in other apartment complexes."

The Chief of Police made a comment, "Thank you Shelly, for coming down from the college and giving us your opinion on these issues." Thank you, my pleasure," said Shelly.

Charles announced "In the next week or so a team of policemen will be canvassing the city doing a door to door search for anyone that does not conform to city standards. They will be equipped with a search warrant and if anything looks suspicious they will be taken to the police station for a routine interview and investigation. If everything is satisfactory they will be released." Goodnight everybody and may God Bless you." Everybody bid the Police Chief "Goodnight."

Next Week…

Monday afternoon finds Deputy Marcus training the policemen for the door to door search for anyone that does not conform to city standards. Most of the people's standards are average, above average and poverty level. The occupants of the poverty level group are predominately different races and nationalities. Some of the people fail to comply with city standards, as a numerous result of cats and dogs are running wild, inside and out, no food for the children and little baby, and dog and cat feces all over the trailer, even on the beds. The children are also running rampant on the streets, with barely any clothes on. The police have already taken them to the police station and will keep them there until someone cleans up the filthy house, buys some food and cleans up the children. The police own two old apartment houses, next to the police station for cases such as these, until the situation has been resolved. There are four apartments in each house and one of the houses is already full.

Transients that live on the street have been removed from the situation and placed in a shelter for men downtown. Other people with similar problems will be placed in a facility according to their needs.

As Charles, the police chief, said one day, "We've fingerprinted the whole city, did a door to door search and improved the quality of life for many people in this city. We have the pit bull for evidence and we're still no closer to finding the killer or killers, than we were the day it happened. We've even had detectives in here from St. Louis several times to scour the countryside in search of clues or leads that will tie us to the killer, to no avail. Nothing seems to work. Maybe we need to intercede to a higher power, namely God. I'll have to work on that. Give me sometime, because I am bogged down with work."

A Week Later...

Charles, the Police Chief, announced at a staff meeting this morning, "All leads and clues have been exhausted, we have reached a dead end with nowhere to go. If we don't come up with something soon the killings will just continue and more innocent people will lose their lives. This is a sad, sad situation. Then again, I wonder, could the killer be walking among us, unrecognized? What do you think, men?"

I'm going to make arrangements on the way home at the parsonage of the Rockwood Community Church with Pastor Hale for a month's long weekly church service to implore God's help in finding the killer, because this has gone on too long already.

As he entered the parsonage Pastor Hale was just leaving, and he stepped back into the office to talk to Charles. Charles explained the whole situation and Pastor Hale checked his services for the next month and said, "I can accommodate the public every Wednesday evening for the next month at 7:00 PM for a service imploring God's grace and help in this difficult time in our community. A small sermon and music will be included." Charles accepted that, thanked Pastor Hale and left.

*BLOOD SUCKING SERIES NO. 1: THE FINAL FLOOR*

The first service is scheduled for tomorrow night at Rockwood Community Church a 7:00 p.m. As fall is fast approaching, people are wearing jackets and driving their cars instead of walking. The weather has turned remarkably cooler for September 4$^{th}$. Birds are flying south for the winter in droves, flowers once blooming are drying up, bushes, grass and trees look weathered and void of any real color. People are pouring into church well ahead of the designated time to get a place to sit for the hour long service. At 6:30 PM the church is practically full with people standing against the walls and chairs being brought in. Some people are standing outside for the service, with a speaker piped out so they can join in the prayers and song. Pastor Hale gave an emotional sermon about all the misfortune that has taken place since Fern Taylor's death in 1995, and all the deaths following. Pastor Hale made the comment from the pulpit, "Sometimes God can take years, yes, I mean years to answer our prayers, but he does answer them. In my experience, I know that when it comes to answering our prayers, God answers you positively and sometimes not so positively, or he gives you the strength to cope with whatever he puts before you. Sometimes it might take a long, long time."

Communal prayers were said after the sermon and music followed. A collection was taken up and more music followed. People began to file out of church, as it was well attended. Everybody said they would be back next Wednesday night for another service. Police Chief, Charles, thanked Pastor Hale and left also.

Nothing miraculous happened after the public's intercession to God for help during this difficult time the city of Rockwood is going through in regards to the continuous killings since the first death of Fern Taylor in 1995.

A Week Later…

Once again, it's Wednesday evening and time for service at Rockwood Community Church at 7:00 PM.

Charles, his wife Alice, Marcus and a group of policemen in uniform are sitting in the front pew. All the tenants from the Rockwood Apartment

Complex are present and also students from the Rockwood College. Also present are workers from the Animal Shelter plus a variety of people from the city of Rockwood.

The church again is filled to capacity, the pews are full and people are standing against the wall. Chairs are being brought in to accommodate the overflow of people this evening. The usual collection is taken up, followed by the whole congregation joining in hymns of praise to our Almighty God. Pastor Hale dismisses the assembly of people, with a reminder of the services next week Tuesday at 7:00 PM. Everybody smiles, nods their heads and proceeds toward the doors of the church. They are met by a cool breeze and a slight drizzle as they walk to their cars to go home.

A group of tenants from the Rockwood Apartment Complex made arrangements to meet at Dan's Diner for coffee and conversation, before they retired to their apartments across the street.

# CHAPTER 16
# A QUIET LIFE

2001-2002

Nothing to spark anyone's interest as no new leads or clues have surfaced in regards to the succession of murders at the Rockwood apartment Complex. Life goes on, but rarely a day goes by that these innocent victims are not thought of by the local people.

Seasons come and go, as everybody goes about their own business, working, playing, whatever it takes to lead a full productive life. Life will never be back to normal in this city of 12,479 residents because of the dark cloud of murder that hangs over the city, upper most in everyone's mind. The police are patrolling the streets more than usual, fewer people are seen walking on the streets at night and the city parks are empty after the sun sets. Less people are in the stores in the evening, as the night traffic has been reduced to a minimum. People are hesitant to be out after dark, because of all the murders that have occurred at the Rockwood Apartment Complex and otherwise. The people that are usually out after dark are the tenants that drive to the downtown restaurants and Dan's Diner for coffee, meetings and conversation. Also the church going people that attend services at the Rockwood Community Church on Wednesday nights.

## Christmas—2001

A light snow is beginning to fall as the shoppers are scurrying to their cars with packages in tow, anxious to arrive home and start wrapping them, since tomorrow night is Christmas Eve. Christmas trees, adorned with colored lights, decorate the boulevard in downtown Rockwood. Brightly lit trees also present themselves in the picture windows of the department stores and other businesses. Christmas carolers are going caroling from one store to the next, with steamy hot chocolate and Christmas cookies as their treat. They also stand on the street corners, circling a street lamp, and carol for the enjoyment of the people passing by to listen. Children are screaming and laughing as a horse drawn carriage with a rider, saunters to a stop, letting the children out of the carriage, while a new group crawls in. Fun! Fun! Fun!

## Christmas Eve—2001

Hearken! The church bells of the Rockwood Community Church are pealing to the music of "Silent Night" as worshippers are streaming into the church for the 8:00 PM evening services.

Let's go a little farther north, to the Rockwood Apartment Complex where a Christmas party is in progress. Marcus entered the recreation parlor with a covered dish of potato salad, two wrapped Christmas gifts, a big smile and a hearty appetite, as did everybody else. There was an exchange of formalities, Christmas greetings and their gift exchange. Wrapping paper and ribbons were strewn on the tables and even on the floor, as the tenants scrambled to open their gifts from each other, with a limit of $10.00. Sounds like fun.

Marcus' gift went to Sue; fragrant cologne which she told him was her favorite. Sue's mother, Jane received a kitchen towel set from Rich's wife, Lila, which Jane said, "Would always come in handy."

Everybody started walking up and down the pot luck supper table to partake of the delicious casseroles, salads, desserts and drinks. Friendship and laughter ruled the supper tables, until it was time to join in the Christmas carols. Santa Claus entered the scene joking and

*BLOOD SUCKING SERIES NO. 1: THE FINAL FLOOR*

laughing and distributing snacks to anybody with a sweet tooth. About 10:00 PM the Christmas party came to a close and everybody said goodnight and picked up their remaining dishes and gifts and went to their apartments. Marcus also went home, as a light snow had begun to fall, adding to the eleven inches that were already on the ground, making everything look like a picture post card at Christmas time.

Marcus arrived home about 10:30 PM, watched a little television and then went to bed. He will get up early on Christmas morning to go to the Rockwood Community Church for Christmas Day Service at 10:00 AM with his friends from the Rockwood Apartment Complex and downtown for dinner as a few restaurants are open on Christmas Day.

Everybody met in the vestibule of the Rockwood Community Church and proceeded to sit as a group in the pews, close to the sanctuary. Pastor Hale conducted the service with communal prayers, a sermon and singing to follow. A collection was taken up and services ended with the beautiful "Silent Night." The group from the apartment complex all met at the Star Restaurant for Christmas dinner. The menu, fit for a king, included roasted turkey, mashed potatoes, gravy, dressing, corn, cranberry sauce, rolls, salads, pie and drinks. Everybody ate and visited to their hearts content and then they all went home for the day.

Marcus drove back to his apartment and decided to call Betty to see how she's doing at the Women's Prison in Plattsville, Illinois. Marcus placed the call and said, "Betty, this is Marcus. How are you? I thought I'd call and wish you a Merry Christmas and Happy New Year. It's been quite awhile since I called you." Betty answered, "How good to hear your voice, Marcus. I'm glad you called. Merry Christmas and Happy New Year to you. Everything's the same since day one. I still work in the laundry department here at the women's prison. They keep us very busy. I'm up at 5:00 AM in the morning and work until 6:00 PM in the evening. I'm very tired at the end of the day. I've met some nice women friends that I communicate with. Actually, I work with them in the laundry department. One is from Bixby, Illinois and the other two are from the St. Louis area. Are you still keeping busy at the college, Marcus?" Marcus said, "Yes, they keep me very busy. I'm also Assistant Deputy at the Rockwood Police Department, so I put in some long hours. I like both of my jobs and I make good money. That's what I really like, the money." Betty said, "I'm counting the days till I get out of this prison., From today, I have about 323 days left, almost a year. I can't wait to get out of this crappy place. I got myself into a terrible mess with Mary and Ella. It was all my own fault and now I'm having to pay for it."

Marcus replied, "That's right, Betty. I'm sure you've learned your lesson by now. Guess I'll have to hang up now. Betty, because it's getting late. I'll call you again sometime. Goodbye."

Betty said, "Goodbye, Marcus," and hung up. Marcus went on to bed, because he had to get up early to go to work at the college.

Christmas is over and New Years Day is a repetition of Christmas, where the same group will get together for church services and then a meal at the Star Restaurant. After that they will go back to the apartment complex, watch television and then retire for the evening. Or some might go to the recreation parlor for a quick game of billiards, some coffee, a little television, or some light conversation. Some residents like to watch the weather forecast for the next day, in case they have something planned or somewhere to go. It's always better to have something to do, right?

### January 2002

A new year is beginning, hoping that it will be better than the last years have been. It's a quiet life these days, nothing going on and in the dead of winter.

Marcus continues to play Pinochle every Tuesday at the Rockwood Apartment Complex and goes to church services on Wednesday evening with the group from the apartments. The church services have been going on for almost two years, with still no clues or leads as to the killer of the victims at the apartments.

The pit bull still continues to live at the animal shelter, until the killer is brought to justice. Basically everything else is the same.

## Valentine's Day, February 14th

Valentine's Day is making a swift entry and a fast exit. One day Rich announced to the Pinochle group, "We are going to have a Valentine's Day party for all the residents of the complex with an exchange of Valentine cards, a pot luck supper and a variety of treats."

Tuesday is the first Valentine party that the complex has ever had since it is open. The residents enter the recreation parlor with their casserole dishes, salads, desserts, etc. The men have their Valentine cards tucked neatly in their pockets, while the ladies carry them in their purses.

Everybody partakes of the Valentine supper, and then exchanged their cards, nibbling on treats all night long. Conversation ensued about the latest gossip, news and weather. After that everybody bid each other goodnight and went back to their apartment.

Marcus drove home in a howling snowstorm that he could barely see out of the windshield. He almost hit another car on the way home, because of all the snow that covered the other car. The other car was barely visible.

When Marcus walked into his apartment he noticed that his answering machine was blinking and he immediately checked it. Marcus' brother, Adam, started talking to him and telling him that their mother had a bad stroke and Doctor Zine said, "Your mother is just hanging on yet, like she's waiting to see Marcus. It's just a matter of half a day, maybe not even that." When Marcus heard that, he was all upset and he started wiping his tears, saying to himself out loud, "I'll make a few telephone calls, get ready and be on my way tonight yet."

Marcus called the complex and spoke to Rich, telling him, "My mother is dying of a stroke, and I'm leaving for St. Louis tonight yet, so I won't be at the Wednesday night Pinochle game. I should be back in three or four days.

Marcus immediately called Charles, the police chief, and told him what had happened. He said, "I'll be gone for three of four days, maybe longer. My mother is near the end of her life, and I won't come back until everything's over." The police chief said, "The police department extends their sympathy and we want you to take as much time off as you need, Marcus. We'll see you when you get back. Have a safe trip up and back."

Marcus then called to the home of his supervisor at the college and explained the situation to him and he said the same thing as the police chief said, "The Rockwood College extends its sympathy and we want you to stay as long as its necessary, Marcus. Your job will be waiting for you when you get back."

After Marcus was finished with his telephone calls he proceeded to take a shower, pack his suitcase, and was on his way by 11:00 PM. He figured he would be in St. Louis by 11:00 AM the next morning. He also stopped at an all night diner to drink some coffee, so he would stay awake and it worked. It was past midnight February 15, with a light snow falling as Marcus continued driving, listening to the music coming from an all night St. Louis radio station KSIB.

Marcus drove all night long, except to stop for gas and breakfast and a look at the local newspaper, namely, for the weather forecast, which called for continued heavy snow. When he left he asked the cashier, "How close am I to St. Louis?" And they said, "About 300 miles straight east." Marcus said, Thank you," and left.

Finally around 11:00 AM Marcus arrived at the only home he and his siblings have ever known. Adam, his brother, and his two sisters, Vivian and Clare came out to greet him and explain to him that he must go to the hospital immediately, because his mother was asking for him all day. So they left for the hospital, midst heavy snow by this time. When they arrived in Marcus' mother's room, she was awake and said, "Marcus, Marcus, my son. I've been waiting for you all day." Marcus asked, "How are you, Mom?" She replied, "Oh so, I don't really know what I'm up here for. I just got sick all of a sudden and they brought me to the hospital and called you. How was the weather coming up here?" Marcus said, "It was snowing lightly all the way, and now it's a lot heavier."

All of a sudden there was no answer. Marcus heard a gurgling sound and then he heard his mother take one last breath as she passed away. Marcus was shocked since he'd never been in the presence of anyone that had died before. Adam, Clare and Vivian were also in the room, but they had experienced their father's death in this way, because he died at home.

The casket was open the next day for several hours viewing at the New Found Baptist Church that Marcus remembers attending while he was still at home. Ann, Marcus' mother, looked beautiful in the casket in her pale blue dress, with her hair neatly coiffed and a soft smile on her face. After church services the body was buried at the St. Louis cemetery, with many friends and relatives present.

They had a heavy lunch in the church basement for their out of town relatives, friends and local acquaintances. Marcus ate lunch and then slept most of the day, so he could leave early the next morning, since it was a long drive back to Rockwood Illinois.

After bidding farewell to Adam, Clare and Vivian, Marcus left St. Louis, Missouri at 7:00 AM in the morning with the weather clear and cold, 5 degrees above zero. At least it wasn't snowing. Except, the farther east he drove, the deeper the snow got, plus he witnessed numerous cars being pulled out of snow banks along Interstate 70, with the highway patrol telling him, "Interstate 70 is glazed with ice and is closed from here to Illinois state line. Sir, you will have to take this detour to get back on to Interstate 14, which will also get you to the Illinois state line. Have a safe trip, Sir." Marcus said, "Thank you," and drove the course the highway patrolman suggested. When he reached Interstate 14, the highway was clear of snow and ice and the amount of snow didn't seem quite as much, so Marcus proceeded to finish the last leg of his trip. Marcus isn't far from Rockwood, Illinois, with very little snow and not such a bitter cold welcoming him.

When Marcus arrived back he called the police chief to tell him he would be in to work the next afternoon at 3:00 PM, after he got off work at the college. He also called his janitorial supervisor telling him. "Mr. Mills, this is Marcus and I'm back from my trip and I'll be in to work at 7:00 a.m. in the morning." To which Mr. Mills replied, "Fine, I'll look forward to seeing you, Marcus."

Marcus that same night, called the Women's Prison in Plattsville, Illinois to talk to his girlfriend, Betty. When she answered, Marcus said,

"Hello, Betty, this is Marcus, remember me? I didn't get a chance to tell you because I left for St. Louis at 11:00 PM at night and it would've been too late to call you. My mother died of a stroke, we buried her and I just got back." Betty said, "Marcus, I extend my deepest sympathy in the death of your mother. I'm sure she's in a better place." Marcus talked to Betty for a few minutes and then he hung up. He knows he has to get up at 6:00 AM in the morning to be at work at 7:00 AM.

Marcus was at work at the college at 7:00 AM in the morning the next day. After he got off work at 3:00 PM he worked as a deputy for the Rockwood Police Department.

Marcus was anxious to play Pinochle with his friends at the complex, since he missed last week because of his mother's funeral in St. Louis. When they were all seated, everybody began questioning Marcus about his trip. Rich spoke for the group saying, "Marcus, we offer our condolences upon the death of your mother. We are glad you are back amongst us again, safe and sound. We missed you last week." Marcus said, "I thought of everybody playing Pinochle the night I was driving to St. Louis in the bad, snowy weather."

Sue asked, "How did you find your family, Marcus" Marcus announced, "Very well, in spite of what happened to my mother. My nieces and nephews are growing like weeds. Three of them are in high school and one is in college. It makes me feel old, even though I'm not." Jane also asked Marcus a question, "Marcus, is there a lot of traffic late at night and do you stop at rest stops along the way?" Marcus said, "No, there's not as much traffic on the highway at night like there is during the day. I stopped several times going up and coming back for gas and to eat my meals. They have plenty of rest stops and restaurants along the way, especially when you get to the edge of the city."

Rich and Lila provided the snacks for the evenings Pinochle game which consisted of peanut butter cookies and hot tea for a change. At 10:00 PM the pinochle game was over and everyone bid everyone else "goodnight" and went back to their apartment. Marcus got in his car, drove back to his apartment and went to bed for the night. Tomorrow came bright and early.

*BLOOD SUCKING SERIES NO. 1: THE FINAL FLOOR*

t Rockwood College yesterday, which bussed
xtra college students for hands on training in
There would be a lot of extra cleaning for
tors in the classrooms, halls and the variety of
as. One thousand extra students can account
al work.
rting for his deputy job, because of his extra
1 he did report for work, they were swamped
ies that transpired over the last several days
of a deputy, for which Marcus was trained.
at the college, he will also work late at his
partment, at least until 11:00 PM.

# Chapter 17
# Escaping Gas

At the last Pinochle game Rich announced, "The complex will be having our annual Irish Day Party for those who are of Irish descent. Those who are not Irish may still attend. There is also a note on our bulletin board in regard to this. We will have an Irish pot luck supper, some singing and games, which will start at 6:00 PM. Please observe this day as many of you are of Irish descent. Thank you."

On Thursday night of the Irish pot luck supper one could smell Irish stew, corned beef, cabbage and other Irish delicacies casseroles and pastries cooking and baking, up and down the hall.

Around 5:30 PM Rich Burns and his wife Lila and Pearl Biller got on the elevator on the fourth floor to go to the recreation parlor for the Irish Day Party. As the elevator closed, it made a humming sound after they selected the main floor and it didn't start. Rich pushed the main floor number again and it started humming. They waited a little while and repeated the process and then there was an even louder humming, but no movement. For a minute, Pearl said, "I think I smell something different, although I can't identify the odor. To me, it smells like rotten eggs. I recognize that smell from at home years ago in the chicken house. Rich don't you and Lila smell anything at all? It could possibly be something else, I don't know. Who knows?

Maybe I'm imagining things." Rich pushed the select button for the recreation parlor again, and still no movement, but the humming had now quit. Lila and Rich sniffed and smelled the same odor as Pearl, a foul smelling odor, similar to rotten eggs. Lila realized what it was and screamed, "Its gas! We are being gassed. Pearl was crying and Rich was screaming and beating the new, sound proof elevator doors and walls with no response. "Help, Help! We're getting gassed! Get someone please. The elevator doesn't open! Something's terribly wrong! We are going to die if someone doesn't get help soon! There's gas escaping from somewhere! Please push the button on the outside panel, please!" All of a sudden a thump was audible as Lila slumped to the floor. Rich was the next person that succumbed to the deadly gas fumes, as he lay on the elevator floor struggling for air and literally turning blue in the process. Pearl started to vomit as she turned an ashen gray color. She stopped breathing as her frail body lay twisting, writhing and gasping her last breath.

Lila still conscious crawled over the bodies of Rich and Pearl to the select button and raked her fingers over the panel. Not pushing any button in particular, she lost her grip, and her fingers slid down as she collapsed to the floor. By this time Lila is lying on her back, her eyes rolled back in her head with a fixed stare, as death is creeping upon her. But all of a sudden she regurgitates and bile and frothy vomit gush out of her mouth, with a stench that is unbearable. Her body twisting and writhing in pain and convulsive reaction frees itself of its agony and grief.

Rich, Lila and Pearl have lost their lives to a serial killer once again. In the meantime, the tenants are preparing to partake of their pot luck supper, when Marcus inquired, "Where are Rich, Lila and Pearl this evening? That's strange! There all three of Irish descent and they said they were definitely coming. I guess I'll go and check up on them. Excuse me for a little bit." Marcus went to the lobby for the third floor, but the elevator never came down. Marcus thought that was odd, so he pushed it again and still no response, so he decided to take the back stairs to the third floor. When he reached the third floor, he immediately saw the elevator, but he couldn't get it to move either way. He also smelled the rotten egg odor and he knew immediately what it was, and he had a good idea who was in the elevator.

He quickly called the maintenance repairman for the complex. Mr. Legg came quickly, working on the elevator door until it opened up.

There lay the dead bodies of Rich and Lila Burns and Pearl Biller, their bodies already swollen and bathed in sweat. Lila's eyes are still open with that fixed stare, while Rich and Pearl's eyes are closed.

Marcus was so overcome with grief because he had just buried his mother and now three of his best friends are dead. Marcus mustered the strength and courage somehow to go downstairs and tell the group what had happened.

When he came into the recreation parlor they all sensed something terrible had taken place. Especially, when they heard the police sirens going outside of the complex and the front doors open and policemen, detectives and paramedics all over the place.

After Carl Biller was notified and struck with grief, almost to the point of being hospitalized, he was beside himself with anger also. He said, "I swear I'll move out of this damn apartment and I feel like suing the Rockwood Apartment Complex for losing my wife. This is unbelievable. It's disgusting!"

After they were told what had happened they were all crying and stricken with grief and many said, "I'm moving out of here as soon as I get myself another apartment. That makes seven people dead already since these killings first started. I'm scared. No sane person will want to live in here." Mrs. Rigby said, "I was warned about this place and now I'm getting out of these devil's quarters. I wonder if this place isn't possessed by the devil." Mr. Millow is a new comer to the apartments and he said he'd heard rumors about the complex and ignored it. He hasn't finished unpacking and he doesn't think he will. He said, "I'm going to check the other apartments for rent and move out of here. I've had enough already. I wonder if this complex won't get condemned later on. It should!"

As they were speaking some of the policemen came over to the group to question them as the paramedics carried them out the door on gurneys into the waiting ambulance, headed for the hospital.

Marcus and several other detectives were still in the elevator looking for fingerprints, clues anything they could tie to the murders.

Mr. Legg is having the Metropolitan Gas Company come by in the morning and check the gas leak and see what happened, since the gas was coming from the inside of the elevator.

The Next Morning...

The Metropolitan Gas Company and detectives arrived at 8:00 AM and proceeded to investigate where the gas was seeping into the elevator from. They started the elevator numerous times; going down to the main floor and then back as far as it will go, to the sixth floor, with no recurrence of the problem. They checked other mechanical aspects of the elevator, but everything seemed to be in working order. The elevator door is in working condition and there was no reason the elevator didn't open, other than a slight malfunction in the controls which was checked and is fine. Did something snap shut by accident? Something caused this, Right? The Metropolitan Gas Company said, "We have not been able to detect where the gas is seeping into the elevator from. Gas detectors are being positioned at the base of the elevator floor to pick up the odor of gas, but so far, no odor has been detected. The detectives said, "We are looking for fingerprints again, in case we missed something the first time, but none have been found.

Rich and Lila Burns and Pearl Biller's families have been notified about the deaths of their loved ones and plan to arrive sometime today.

Rich was a carpenter by trade and Lila was a health nurse, both having retired five years ago. They are both from Rockwood, Illinois and have four children, Bob, Joan, Phyllis and Ray. Two live in Indianapolis, Indiana and two live in Washington, D.C. They have seven grandchildren.

Pearl Biller's husband Carl, 87, is devastated at the thought of losing Pearl. Her family arrived today and took him to his family doctor for an injection to help him cope with the impact of it all. Carl seems to be doing much better now. Pearl is survived by one daughter Ellen from

Virginia City, Virginia and three grandchildren. Carl was an accountant and Pearl, a homemaker. Both are from Bixby Illinois.

Public viewing of Rich and Lila Burns and Pearl Biller will be tonight at 7:00 PM at the Brown Mortuary. Rich and Lila Burns will be in one room and Pearl Biller in another. The room of Rich and Lila is filled to overflowing as the mourners offer their sympathy to their families and view the bodies. Rich is clad in a navy blue suit, his hair neatly combed and a faint smile on his face. His wife, Lila, is dressed in a pink dress, her hair beautifully coiffed with a peaceful look on her face.

In the next room is Pearl Biller, wearing a black dress, her hair stylishly arranged with a quiet, reserved demeanor. Pearl's room is full to capacity with people waiting in the hallway to view the body. Friends and relatives file past the casket and then offer their condolences to their families. Pastor Hale conducted a small prayer filled service.

The First Southern Baptist Church was the scene the next day of the funeral of Rich and Lila Burns at 10:00 AM. The church was filled to the point of overflowing, as chairs were set in the hallways.

Pearl Biller's funeral service was at the United Methodist Church at 10:30 AM the same day.

After the funeral services were over all three bodies were brought to Rockwood Cemetery, their final resting place. There was a huge attendance at the burials because everybody knew Rich, Lila and Pearl. They had many friends and acquaintances and were well thought of.

A luncheon in memory of Rich and Lila followed in the biggest hall in Rockwood which was the Bricker Hall on the south edge of town. A luncheon for Pearl Biller was in the basement of the United Methodist Church, which was well attended. All the relatives and friends of Rich and Lila Burns and Pearl Biller went home with saddened hearts.

Before Carl Biller's daughter and family left, she decided that they would be back to transfer Carl to the Southern Heights Nursing Home in Rockwood because of the safety factor and his inability to fend for himself any longer. Ellen said, "He needs to be in a different environment with a circle of friends and maybe he would have a different attitude. I will check with the nursing home for the first available vacancy, before

I leave. My dad is looking forward to leaving since Fern Taylor's death in 1995.

Mr. George Millow is moving to another apartment complex in town next week Monday. It didn't take him long to find an apartment. He was anxious to leave because of the fear gripping him and all of the tenants. Mr. Millow said, "Every time you step in the elevator you don't know whether you'll be alive when the elevator stops."

Mrs. Faye Rigby is also moving to another apartment in about two weeks, as soon as the residents vacate the apartment. After Fern was killed she didn't like it at the complex anymore. And now she's getting out. She was known to say to other tenants, "I should have gotten out way before this got so bad."

Marcus decided to call Betty this evening since he hadn't talked to her for awhile. When Betty picked up the phone, Marcus said, "Hello Betty, this is Marcus." How are you? I've been meaning to call you for sometime now, but we've had a lot going on around here. Maybe you read about it in the newspaper, the three people that got gassed in the elevator on St. Patrick's Day, just before the Irish Pot Luck Supper. It was awful. Rich and Lila Burns and Pearl Biller died in the elevator asphyxiated with gas. Mr. Legg and I, the elevator maintenance man were the first to arrive upon the scene right after it happened." Betty said, "Yes, I saw that in the paper. What a shock for the other tenants at the complex. And it sounds like they don't have any clues as to where the gas came from inside the elevator. That's strange, all those killings sound odd, Marcus. The pit bull murders, the snake, someone was shot to death, the gassings. I've never heard of such odd, strange deaths and especially in an elevator.

A person would think they would be safe in an elevator. I guess not necessarily. It just makes me scared to want to go in an elevator. How about you Marcus? Are your scared?"

Marcus said, "Well, I'm sure going to be extra careful from now on. Actually, I'm probably going to be taking the back stairs from now on, where it's safer. I need the exercise anyway." Betty said, "You'd better be careful, Marcus. I don't want to see your name in the paper as a victim. That would be terrible. Marcus, do you ever see my parents anymore?

If you do, tell them I'll be calling pretty soon. I have something to tell them." Marcus said, "No, it's been a long time since I've seen them. I'll tell them what you said, Betty, Okay, Marcus, bye."

Marcus said, "Bye, Betty," and hung up the phone. He watched television for awhile, took his nightly shower and then went to bed.

### Tuesday Night—Pinochle

Marcus had Tuesday night off, so he decided to play Pinochle with his friends at the complex, those that are left, that is. Sue and her mother, Jane, Carl Biller moved to another apartment in town, Dorothy McGuire, Millie Lyons, and Adam Arbison. Dorothy, Millie and Adam are new recruits. Marcus asked the new card players to introduce themselves and they did, Dorothy said, "I'm Dorothy McGuire and I've lived at the complex 2 years, in spite of all the sad things that have been happening. My husband, Mike, is deceased and I'm retired from being a school principle."

Millie Lyon's said, "Hi, I'm Millie Lyons. I've lived at the complex four years. My husband, Dan, isn't well and stays in the apartment most of the time watching television. I'm retired from the secretarial position I had for forty years."

Adam Arbison said, "Hello, I'm Adam Arbison and I've lived here at the complex for six years. My wife died 8 years ago and I'm retired from the mechanic business. We don't have any children."

Marcus said, "Well, we all welcome you to our little Pinochle group. My name is Marcus Reil and this is Sue Benson and her mother Jane Linton. We play Pinochle here every Tuesday night at 7:00 PM for something to pass the time. They played Pinochle till 10:00 PM with Marcus' team winning. Every once in awhile someone started a light conversation such as Jane, with a question, "Marcus, how are you doing with the murder investigations yet? Any new clues or leads?" Marcus replied, "No Jane, were at a standstill with everything. The detectives from St. Louis aren't any better than we are. They couldn't find anything either. It's so aggravating. If we knew who was doing these killings we might be shocked." Jane replied, "Yes, we might be."

As everybody got up to leave Marcus said, "I suggest everybody take the back stairs to your apartment. It's safer." And they all did. Marcus drove back to his apartment.

## Wednesday—Church

The next night Marcus and his friends from the apartment complex met at the Rockwood Community Church for services conducted by Pastor Hale. After services the complex group meets at the LaBamba Restaurant in downtown Rockwood for coffee and conversation. Those attending the coffee are Marcus, Dorothy, Millie, Jane, Sue, Adam, Dan Blythe, Don Murke and numerous other tenants. Various issues were discussed, as Marcus said, "It's getting late, so we'd all better head back home. I suggest the complex tenants take the back stairs for the time being. We don't want to encourage anything."

A slow rain was coming down as Marcus left the apartment complex, headed for home. After he came home, he kicked off his shoes and dropped into the recliner to relax, because he didn't have to work tonight either.

Marcus called Betty's parents and inquired how they were and told them he had talked to Betty about a week ago and that Betty would be calling them soon. They were glad to hear that and thanked Marcus whole heartedly. They also invited Marcus to their home for a meal where they live. Marcus said he would call them in advance when he was coming. Marcus also called his boss Charles and told him, it was sure nice of you to give me two nights off in a row. That way I could play Pinochle with my friends and go to church and out to coffee with them the next night. That way I can always keep in touch with my friends, which I'm doing anyway. Charles said, "I'm glad you enjoyed yourself Marcus."

Marcus was extra busy at the college today because the students were having another event to commemorate a milestone. So there was extra cleaning to do.

Marcus was very tired, so he showered and went to bed. He fell asleep with a light, drizzly rain in the back ground, but was awakened by a loud clap of thunder and lightening. He quickly got up and ran to the window to watch the rain come down in torrents, filling Poller Street and the other surrounding streets. It was curb to curb and it looked like it was coming into basement windows. Marcus turned the television on and listened as the announcer said Poller Street and the surrounding streets were flooding fast. Marcus had an upstairs apartment, but even so he didn't like the idea of everything flooding. He grabbed some bedding and drove through water to the apartment complex and spent the night on the blue divan in the recreation parlor, just like old times.

## Chapter 18
## Evacuation II—May

The next morning Marcus is up bright and early, so that he can run across the street to Dan's diner to eat breakfast before he goes to work. The waitress asked Marcus, "Did you get flooded out?" He said he doesn't know because he left his apartment while it was still flooding.

Now, he is getting ready to go back again. He drove up to Poller Street and the surrounding area to evaluate the flooding conditions, which was all under water where he lived.

Classes at Rockwood College have been cancelled, because the college is surrounded by water and no one can get into the college because of the flooding. Marcus is planning on staying in the complex lobby because he can't get into his apartment until the water recedes. He will have to continue to sleep on the couch and eat at Dan's Diner.

Surprisingly, the water receded fast and Marcus was able to get to work at the college and into his apartment. While he was at the complex one night, he decided to take the elevator to the sixth floor to check on the back stairs. When he got into the elevator he got a faint whiff of rotten eggs (namely gas) and he immediately stopped the elevator, because he knew there was something wrong again. He called Mr. Legg and had them contact the Metropolitan Gas Company again. Besides the Metropolitan Gas Company coming out and checking they also called another gas company to help along, namely, The Western Gas Company. They would assist in the investigation and give their second opinion.

In the morning all the residents evacuated to Dan's Diner for the duration of the time it takes for the gas companies to complete their work. The residents will be in the diner most of the day, playing cards, visiting and eating their meals. The residents that are not at the diner went shopping for the day and some went to their relatives in the city. The Pinochle players are playing with two sets of teams. Jane, Sue and Marcus on one team and Dorothy, Millie and Adam on another team, with Jane's team always winning.

After supper about 7:00 PM, one of the workers from the "Western Gas Company" came over to the diner and said, "All the residents can go back into their apartments now because everything's been checked and we can't find any fault with the gas system. Everything checked out okay. The gas odor must've been put in the elevator by the killer somehow, because we checked the flooring and no gas came through from underneath the floor of the other side of the elevator. Is it possible that the gas odor that Marcus smelled could be the odor that killed three people and then resurfaced once in awhile, but not strong enough to kill anybody?"

The residents arose, gathered their belongings and proceeded to leave for the Rockwood Apartment Complex across the street, secure in knowing for a fact, that the complex is safe to go back into. The residents are using the elevator once again with no problems, as it is working, stopping and starting when it's supposed to, no delays, nor jerky movements. A few of the residents still chose to take the back stairs and that's fine.

## The Next Day

Between Marcus' janitorial job and his deputy job, Marcus quickly dashed into the lobby of the apartment complex and posted a notice on the bulletin board about a meeting for the complex residents to co-ordinate the activities this evening at 7:00 PM.

*BLOOD SUCKING SERIES NO. 1: THE FINAL FLOOR*

Many of the residents showed up at 7:00 PM for the meeting conducted by Marcus. He went over the agenda of the activities for the next six months. The first activity on the agenda is Millie's 85$^{th}$ birthday party, next Friday afternoon, complete with cake and ice cream and a dance. Everybody said, "A dance! How are we going to dance in here? There's no room!" Marcus said, "We'll make room. We're going to push the furniture to the side or put it in another room and we'll have the extra space we need, that's how!" Marcus went down the agenda and announced and planned other birthday parties, July 4$^{th}$ party, another birthday party and a Halloween party, plus more. He also announced, "Men, listen up. We need more of you men to come down to the dance, so your wives will have someone to dance with, Okay? And ladies, if your husbands won't come, just go and help yourself. Find someone else to dance with. All the ladies were in very much agreement with that.

Tuesday Night Card Game

Everybody is congregating in the recreation parlor for their weekly card game. Sue, Jane, Marcus, Adam, Dorothy, and Millie are seated at two tables ready to play cards and visit.

As usual, Sue asks Marcus, "How is the murder investigation coming along, Marcus? Any new clues or leads into the different cases? This is a series of murders and you are working with a serial killer, Marcus. Be careful, whatever you do. That's dangerous for you."

Jane said, "Maybe we need to get a search team started, including residents and volunteers to help canvas the area around Rockwood again for anything suspicious or unusual. Remember, we did that months ago, although we didn't come up with anything. At least we tried and I think we should do that again."

Marcus was in agreement with everything saying, "No, I'm sorry to say we are at a dead end. Even the special team of detectives they brought in from the St. Louis area had problems with this whole investigation. These murders have everyone stumped."

Millie said, "I can't believe the way the police department canvassed every household and fingerprinted everybody in town and they didn't come up with somebody or something. That's very unusual and the special team of detectives that you just mentioned, Marcus, they would be more qualified in their training, than a regular detective, I would say. Am I correct, Marcus?"

Marcus said, "Yes, your correct, Millie. A special team of detectives would have more hours and "Hands on" training than a regular detective. Since Fern Taylor's death all of these cases have been hard to crack. This serial killer is very adapt at fooling the police department. That's the hard part. Periodically at staff meetings and otherwise we review the different cases and re-evaluate them to see if we can come up with something different or maybe something we missed. What do you do when you've exhausted all avenues and come up with nothing? There's not much you can do, right?" Hopefully, one of these days, something's going to turn up. It better turn up fast, because we don't want to see any more killings. This last time it was a multiple killing. Three dead in the elevator at one time."

Millie asked another question, "Marcus, does the police station think it's all the work of one person or possibly more than one?"

Marcus answered, "That's a good question, Millie. It could be either way. One person is capable of doing this and so are three persons."

Adam asked, "Marcus is it possible that the serial killer lives in a town not to far from here?" Marcus said, "Yes, Adam, that's a strong possibility too. We haven't canvassed other homes in other communities nor fingerprinted them, but we have checked the pit bull and rattlesnake situation out and there weren't any pit bulls or 6 foot long rattlesnakes in either Bixby or Maplesville, Illinois. There were rattlesnakes in out lying communities with zoos, but they were all accounted for. Dorothy made the comment, "Marcus, is it possible, and I hate to ask this question, that the serial killer could be living right here in the apartment complex? Have you ever thought of that?"

Marcus answered, "Yes, we've thought of that and it's highly possible, but not likely, because I and the police department know a lot of residents on a personal basis that live here. We just don't think that's likely here at the apartment complex.

Even during this question and answer period, everybody is still concentrating on their cards and focused on winning. This being the last game of the evening and Adam's snacks of coffee and pound cake are all gone, it's time to shut everything down and proclaim Dorothy's team the winner. Everybody said goodnight and went to their apartment.

## Birthday Party Dance

Millie's 85th birthday party has been re-posted on the bulletin board and Adam is in charge of the arrangements, because Marcus has to work this evening.

Thirty five residents attended Millie's birthday party, bringing gifts and cards and wishing her a "Happy Birthday" with a song. Everybody was served a piece of cake and ice cream with visiting and a dance to follow.

As the tape played the first Waltz, Millie and her husband Don danced together, the only couple on the floor. Don felt better tonight that he had in a long time, so he came along down to join in Millie's birthday party. Couples were on the dance floor all night, in between eating snacks and visiting.

The birthday party was over at 11:00 PM and everyone made the remark that they really enjoyed the party, especially the dancing. They are all looking forward to the next dance.

## Church Services—Wednesday

Wednesday night is church service night at Rockwood Community Church downtown. A large group from the apartment complex attended the services which consisted of prayers, collection, sermon and songs. Marcus has to work every other Wednesday, so he won't be able to attend tonight's service. Pastor Hale gave an interesting and unique sermon, one of its kind, which was enjoyed by all. He repeatedly speaks about, "If your prayers don't get answered, just keep on praying. Don't give up. That's the worst thing you can do. Continue to pray and if it takes years for your prayers to get answered. Know always that God hears and is close to you. He will answer your prayers in his own time, whenever he wishes. Remember this!"

The congregation sat glued to their pews and focused on Pastor Hale's face, knowing good and well, that they all faced trials and tribulations. They know that their prayers weren't answered and they have been to the point of giving up on prayer, until they listened to Pastor Hale's sermon and they were rejuvenated once more.

Pastor Hale dismissed the congregation after the last song and they proceeded to file out of the church.

The apartment complex group meets at the LaBamba Restaurant for coffee and visiting in downtown Rockwood for about an hour and a half and then they go back to their apartments. Upon the recommendation of Marcus, no one walks downtown anymore. They either drive their cars, or take a taxi or the city bus, because of everything that's transpired at the apartment complex. It's not safe for anybody in the city to be out walking at night.

### Complex meeting—Sunday

Marcus posted an important meeting for this coming Sunday, June 7 in the recreation parlor for all the residents of the apartment complex at 2:00 PM. We will be addressing different issues relevant to living at the complex. Refreshments will be served. It will be conducted by Marcus Reil with a question and answer period to follow.

As Sunday afternoon approaches many of the residents are already seated at 1:50 PM while others are just coming in. At two o'clock Marcus starts the meeting with a review of the past rules and regulations. The residents are welcome to use the back stairs anytime if they feel uncomfortable riding the elevator. When going downtown, please don't walk. Continue to ride the taxi, take the city bus or ride in a car.

Also, Marcus said, "The main reason we're having this meeting today is because some residents are coming in quite late in the evening and we have to keep the front door unlocked pretty late. Starting tonight, the front door will be unlocked till 10:00 PM. At 10:00 PM it will be locked until 6:00 AM in the morning. We will give everybody a key and if you come in after 10:00 PM you can unlock the door with the key. Once you are in the complex and the door closes after you, it automatically locks. If you forget your key or lose it, we will also give you a card with a number on it for you to call. Let's hope there are no problems. Any questions? Please raise your hand. Yes, Adam?"

Adam asked, "If we accidentally lock ourselves out, where is the closest telephone?"

Marcus said, "Your closest phone would be your cell phone if you have one on you. If not, Dan's Diner across the street is open till 11:00 PM and there is a telephone booth up the street. So from now on, when you leave please take your key and card with you because it's for your own good. Don't leave home without it. Any more questions? Okay and Thank you. Have a good night."

Marcus passed out the keys and cards and everybody left.

## Rockwood Senior Center

Many of the Rockwood Apartment complex residents go to the Rockwood Senior Center for their noon meal. They either go by car, taxi or city bus and enjoy the outing.

Also many of the residents have season tickets to the Rockwood Community Theater for their live stage plays and other performances. They have consecutive tickets all year round. The residents are never lacking for something to see or do. Now that they have a key and card they have easy access to getting into the complex after 10:00 PM.

Dorothy and Millie came home one rainy night from a play after 10:00 PM and both had forgotten their key, but not the card, because it is something relatively new to remember, and were locked out. They immediately went to Dan's Diner, across the street, which was closed, so they were forced to walk in the rain down the street to the pay phone and call the number on the card. By the time they walked back to the complex, the door was already unlocked. Several residents were still in the recreation parlor watching television when they came in. Dorothy and Millie told them what had happened. "We got locked out and didn't have our key, but we had our card, so we called and they unlocked the door for us." Joe Beale said, "The same thing happened to me the other day. It's a good thing I had my card along, or else I would've been in trouble. Things like this will teach us a lesson to keep our key and card with us at all times. I know that the complex can't keep the front door unlocked till all hours, in light of all the murders that have occurred since Fern Taylor's death in 1995. Too may people would have access to coming into the complex at all hours of the night. Whoever's responsible for these murders that might be the way he's getting into the complex? Who knows?"

Dorothy said, in response, "Some of the residents are sure getting careless with their keys and cards. I don't know why. The other day Millie and I found two keys and two cards lying on that table over by the window, so we picked them up and turned them into the office. Some one else said they found a key on the elevator floor and also turned it in. The office said, "If the residents are losing their keys and cards that readily, we might have to have another meeting, as a reminder for their key and card. By now, too many keys and cards are being turned in as lost or misplaced and residents are coming to the office to retrieve them. The office manager has posted another notice on the bulletin board announcing a meeting to be held August 14$^{th}$, Friday at 7:00 PM. Everybody is encouraged to attend.

When Friday night approached for the meeting, everybody living in the complex attended. It was held in the recreation parlor and it was filled to capacity, with no extra room. Residents were forced to stand in the hallway and speakers were set up there. The office manager, Mr. Snowell conducted the meeting, saying, "I decided it was necessary that we call a meeting to order this evening. We are faced with a grave issue concerning some of the residents and I will get to the point. Not all of the residents, but some of you are getting very careless with your key and cards. Other residents have been turning them into the office and some of them have not been picked up, which means that there are those of you right now who are without a card or key or both. The keys and cards have been found in such places as the elevator floor, desks, on the pot luck tables and other places. These keys and cards were given to you for your safety and should be kept with you at all times. May I suggest, Ladies, your purse is an ideal place for your key and card. Gentlemen, your card would fit nicely into your wallet and your key can be dropped in your pants pocket. None of this should cause any problems. Any questions? Raise your hand, please."

There were no questions, so Mr. Snowell adjourned the meeting, hoping this would take care of the situation.

Within the next couple of weeks the remaining keys and cards were picked up at the office and so far no more cards or keys have been lost or misplaced. Evidently Mr. Snowell's meeting was a good idea.

Not too many residents are going out in the evening anymore, since they are in a rainy season, and the taxi fares have gone up in price. More of the residents are spending time at home in the evening or in the recreation parlor drinking coffee, watching television, visiting with each other or leafing through magazines. Sometimes a group of them get together at someone's apartment to play cards in-between playing Pinochle on Tuesday evenings in the recreation parlor. A few new people have been added to the pinochle game. The more the merrier!

# Chapter 19
# Into the Woods

Police Chief, Charles, tacked a notice onto the bulletin board announcing a search in the woods scheduled for this coming Sunday September 7$^{th}$, starting at 1:00 PM. Anybody is welcome to volunteer to help search for the serial killer that has been on the rampage since Fern Taylor's death in 1995. A lot of the residents at the complex will be participating Sunday, weather permitting, to explore the area for any kind of a clue that would tie in to the murders.

Marcus, the Federal Bureau of Investigation, the local police and other residents will also be assisting. Everybody woke up to a warm, balmy Sunday, a beautiful, typical fall day. Everybody congregated at 1:00 PM at the base of the woods to be deployed with another person to a certain area of the woods, to look for unusual activity or new evidence, not yet discovered. Everybody paired off and would meet back at the starting point in three hours. "If anybody gets lost or needs help, call the number I gave you on your cell phone. Either you or your friend has to have a cell phone today to participate, because it's not a good idea to go into the woods without one. If you are confronted by a wild animal, don't provoke the animal, but instead speak in a gentle voice, all the while, backing away from the animal and have your partner call for help. Okay! Let's pair off

## BLOOD SUCKING SERIES NO. 1: THE FINAL FLOOR

with our partner. Everybody needs to be back at 4:00 PM. Good luck!"

As Adam and John were walking along, scraping the grass and dirt with their walking sticks which everybody was given, they visited and got acquainted. Adam said, "My name is Adam Arbison, My wife died 8 years ago and I'm retired from the mechanic business. In fact, I was in my own business here in Rockwood for 48 years. We have two children, a son that lives in St. Louis, Missouri and a daughter that lives in Denver, Colorado. We also have five grandchildren. Two boys and three girls. How about you, John?"

John modestly replied, "My story's about like yours Adam. My name is John Leer and my wife also died 11 years ago and I'm retired from the grocery business. We owned and operated Leer's Grocery Stores in a town about fifty miles south of here called Milton, Illinois. We have six children, none are around here. Three of our sons live in Las Vegas, Nevada, one of our daughters lives in Arizona and our other two daughters live in Alabama. There all scatterd and I'm here in Rockwood, Illinois."

Adam and John were doing some visiting, but they were also keeping an eye on anything unusual or weird. All of a sudden, John said "I thought I heard a sound like a twig breaking," they both stopped walking and they didn't hear anything anymore, so they proceeded forward. Then they heard the same sound again and they stopped walking once more. Nothing was heard again, so they went onward. In a split second, an angered, raging coyote, baring his teeth stood in their path, daring them to go by. He was snarling and foaming at the mouth, as his eyes were rolling back in his head. He lurched toward John and Adam, as they jumped back. The coyote was aggressive as he snapped at Adam, barely missing his pant leg, as Adam said in a gentle voice, "Back boy, go back." John immediately called the number on the card on his cell phone for help, meanwhile, calmly keeping the wild coyote at bay. In a matter of a few minutes a small rescue squad came and took over, while others led John and Adam to safety. John and Adam said, "Now we see why they want us to have a cell phone and this card. Smart thinking."

Meanwhile, the FBI was involved in a deep search on the other side of Thunder Creek, following some foot prints from a heavy rain several days ago. They followed the footprints for about a quarter of a mile. They ended at a dilapidated, rusty small shack nestled among some trees in a wooded area. They knocked on the door and when they received no answer, they went in and were approached by a burly, small bearded man who said, "Leave me alone. I didn't do anything. What do you want here? Get out of here!"

The FBI men flashed their badge and said, "We just want to ask you a few questions, if we may."

The bearded man said, "Very well, then. But you're getting the hell out of here cause I ain't done nothing wrong. Get it?"

The FBI said, "We've got it. Like I said earlier, we just want to ask you a few questions. What's your name?" To which he replied, "Jake Klum." The FBI proceeded with their questioning, "Do you live in this shack?" To which he said, "Yes, I like it out here, away from city life. I like it by myself. I'm what you call a recluse. Is that okay with you?" They continued to ask him, "Where do you get your food and anything else you need?" He replied, "I come into the city about once every six weeks for supplies and cart it back home."

By this time, the FBI was getting a little suspicious and said, "Would you mind coming with us, Jake? We'd like to visit with you a little more extensively at this time. We'd also like to do some fingerprinting on you and maybe a line up with other prisoners."

Jake said, "I don't like to come along, but I will. Your just wasting your time because I haven't done anything wrong. I don't have anything to be scared of, so I'll go along." They handcuffed him and led him to the police car. They took him to the police station and proceeded to fingerprint him some more, plus interrogation and posing in a police line up with other prisoners. Everything proved negative and the police department took him back to his shack, thanked him, and said, "We're sorry if we inconvenienced you, Jake. We're just doing our job. Bye."

Nothing turned up with everybody volunteering to help search the woods. Nobody saw anything unusual. Adam and John were approached by a mad coyote. Thank God, for their cell phone. The FBI brought a suspicious looking character into town, checked him out and he was fine.

The FBI will leave this coming Friday for their home base. I'm sure they'll be glad to reach home. I know I'd be. All the times the FBI has come for the different types of murders, they have never indicated that they had a new lead clue, or suspect. The FBI and the Rockwood Police Department have done everything to apprehend the serial killer, but nothing has seemed to work out. The killer is keeping a low profile because he hasn't been caught after six years. One of these days something is going to snap. I'll guarantee you!

Next week Sunday at 1:00 PM, everybody is going to volunteer to help search another area where they have never looked and that's a field and Thunder Creek that are east of Rockwood and see if something will show up there.

## Sunday—Search East of Rockwood

Police Chief, Charles, gives explicit instructions, "Everybody span out, two by two, through the fields and along Thunder Creek east of here. Use your cell phone if you are having difficulty with anything. Please, use your walking stick to balance yourself, even if you don't really need it. Stick with your partner and don't wander off from each other. Also, don't touch anything suspicious, because of the fingerprints. Okay, it's 1:00 PM and I want everybody to meet back here at 4:00 PM. Let's get started! Remember, we're having a meeting at the recreation parlor at 7:00 PM tonight. I'd like for everyone to be there."

John and Adam drug Thunder Creek with a net and didn't come up with anything, other than a dead dog that fell into the creek somehow. Everybody else reported nothing different than the week before. At the meeting that night at 7:00 PM Police Chief, Charles, announced, "We've done everything to try and solve these seven murders and so far we haven't had any luck. We've even had the FBI come in and help us and it still hasn't worked out. We are not going to close the cases, by no means, but the police can't constantly sit and try to figure this out, because we have other issues that have to be addressed. If a lead or clue comes up we will follow it. The police department feels like the apartment complex is pretty well protected with your card and key. Just keep doing as you are told.

As the complex residents were told, "It's still dangerous to be out after dark at night, in light of the murders since the death of Fern Taylor in 1995." But thing do happen in spite of everything. Adam Arbison decided he would like to see a movie that was playing at the Rockwood Cinema, so he took a taxi, not driving anymore since his wife died. He enjoyed the movie and took a taxi back to the complex. After Adam paid the taxi driver, he proceeded to dig in his pocket for his key, since it was around 10:30 PM. Adam thought to himself, "Oh no! Where is my key? I always have it in my pants pocket. Oh, my gosh! I forgot to put my key back in when I changed pants, but here's my card. I'll go over and see if Dan's Diner is still open."

Adam crossed the street and tugged at the diner's front door. It was locked and the lights were off. Now, what's he supposed to do? Not only that, it's beginning to rain. Well, Adam thought, "I've still got my card. I'll just go down the street to that pay phone and call the number on the card and they'll unlock the door." So, Adam went to the pay phone, called the number on the card and told them what had happened and they said they would unlock the door right away. They unlocked the door, but poor Adam never made it back. On his way back to the complex, he thought he heard footsteps behind him. Then he dismissed it from his mind thinking, "I'm just imagining things. I'd better get back to the complex. He started walking a little faster, just in case he was not imagining things, and the footsteps behind him kept coming faster." Now, Adam's thinking, "That's a little too close for comfort."

Before Adam realized what was happening he felt a sharp blow to the back of his head and he was out like a light. He had collapsed on the grass, not far from the complex and his head was bleeding profusely. As he regained consciousness, he could feel the moist, sticky, warm blood trickle down the side of his face and onto his chin. His pain at the back of his head was unbearable, so he continued to lay there in a soggy heap, drenched to the bone, while cars went by oblivious of him lying there. Finally a taxi driver stopped and asked him. "Heh, aren't you the same guy that I dropped off at the apartment complex a little while ago." Adam said, "I sure am. Someone knocked me on the back of the head and then robbed me, after I made a call at the pay phone and was on my way back to the complex. I've been laying here ever since. Nobody stopped by to help me."

The taxi driver said, "Here, let me help you up. I'd better get you to the emergency room at the Rockwood Hospital, because your bleeding pretty bad. Drape your arm over my shoulder and I'll get you into the taxi. It's still raining pretty hard. When we get to the hospital I'll call the staff and have them come out with a gurney or wheelchair, whatever it takes, to get you into the emergency room. I'll come along in with you, don't worry." Adam said, "I'm not worried. Between you and the hospital I'm in good hands." Adam was wheeled into the emergency room where the attending physician, Dr. Roberts, examined his head, conducting an MRI (Mirror Resonance Imaging) test to determine the extent of his injury. Results of the test were conclusive, indicating a blood clot in the upper part of the brain. The physician suggested several days of bed rest in the hospital, medication and a monitoring device to monitor the activity of the blood clot.

After they got Adam into the private room, the taxi driver left and reported his findings to the apartment complex office. The management said, "We figured something had happened when he didn't return to the complex, so we called the police and Marcus took over from there. They caught the assailant, not long after it happened, and he'll be in jail for quite awhile. They interviewed him and fingerprinted him in regard to the other complex murders and he proved negative, we were told by Marcus.

Adam's blood clot receded to the point of total elimination. Adam received many concerned residents, visiting from the apartment complex checking on his welfare. He was dismissed and one of the residents that still drive gave him a ride back to his apartment. It'll be quite awhile before Adam ventures out on the street again, especially without a key. He will temporarily be confined to his apartment for the time being, while in the recuperation process.

Several Weeks Later...

Once a month the newspaper carrier collects the money for the delivery of the local newspaper, The Rockwood Flyer. When he came to Adam's door about supper time and knocked, there was no response. "That's odd," The carrier though, "He usually answers the door right away." He knocked again and still no response, so he reported it to the main office and they checked it out. When the management got inside they discovered Adam lying on the floor, unconscious, and barely breathing, with a strange pallor to his face. The immediately called the ambulance and had him taken to the Rockwood Hospital Emergency Room for treatment. The same physician, Dr. Roberts, examined him again, since he remained unconscious, and couldn't speak. Dr. Roberts said, "He'd had a massive stroke and another MRI indicated a huge blood clot on the upper part of the brain which required immediate surgery. If surgery isn't prepared, he will run the risk of another stroke and then death. Surgery is also risky, but at least he might have a chance. Dr. Robert's performed surgery to remove the huge blood clot, but it was too late because death has already set in.

Adam had passed away at 7:47 PM at this point, unbeknown to his friends at the complex. When word got to the apartment complex all the residents were in total shock, as they filed into the recreation parlor for coffee, snacks and discussion to follow.

Everybody from the complex attended the viewing of the body and extended their sympathy to Adam's relatives in mourner's row. Adam was clad in a dark brown suit, white shirt and brown necktie, his thick, gray hair neatly combed, combined with a serene, peaceful look on his face.

His funeral service will be tomorrow morning at 10:00 AM at the United Baptist Church on Spillman Street. Pallbearers will be Marcus, the Chief of Police, Charles, and four other men from the complex. Burial will be in Rockwood Cemetery, beside his wife, Mabel. Following the funeral service in church. Pastor Rhodes announced, "Following the burial there will be a luncheon in the church basement for all the people attending the service and burial, plus local friends, as Adam was well known at the complex having lived there six years. He was also a native of Rockwood and retired from his own business. He was 76 years old.

The funeral luncheon was well represented by his relatives and the Rockwood Apartment Complex residents, office staff and maintenance department and various acquaintances and local friends of Rockwood.

## October 2002

Now that evenings are getting cool, more tenants are staying inside, than going out. Some of the residents are watching television; others are playing cards and drinking coffee. Some are eating a snack, while still others are playing bingo and some are just plain visiting.

The pit bull is still where he's always been, at the Rockwood Animal Shelter with a lot of other dogs. No one has ever come forward to claim the dog, so he continues to live at the animal shelter. This particular night when everybody was congregating in the recreation parlor, Marcus happened to be there and asked everybody if they would like to go on a picnic this Sunday afternoon in Turners Park and everybody said, "Yes!" Marcus designated some residents to bring briquets for the barbecue, potato salad, baked beans, hamburger and hot dog buns, relish, cole slaw, pop and ice cream bars. We will all meet at Turner's Park at 11:00 AM for lunch, so don't eat lunch at home.

## Sunday, October 17

Sunday finally arrived and the whole complex came to Tuner's Park for lunch. Everybody brought a dish, buns or something to complete the lunch. After they ate they sat and visited, some played catch, and others played horseshoes. Some had not played horseshoes since they were in grade school. Dorothy and Millie enjoyed playing horseshoes. Millie said, "I remember the first time I ever played horseshoes. I lost the game, but it was the most fun I ever had. Remember those days, Dorothy?" Dorothy said, "Oh! I remember very well. That was my favorite game, even though I didn't ever win. Those were the good old days." They both said, "We'll have to do this again sometime." They all spent the afternoon in the park and were back in the apartment when it got dark.

Monday night at the complex is <u>BINGO</u> night, with $1.00 prizes to be given away. Millie is the bingo caller and it starts at 7:00 PM and is over at 10:00 PM.

There are lots of activities at the complex to attend, if a person just wants to. Many of the residents take a taxi or a night bus, about six at a time and go to the Rockwood College for a play or basketball game. Some of the residents go bowling downtown and stop at LaBamba's Restaurant for a quick coffee before they head home before dark. May take walks during the day when the weather is pleasant.

Like Marcus said, "We'll have to have lunches like this more often, because it seems like we all enjoyed it." To which everyone replied, "Yes, lets do this more often because there won't be many nice, warm, fall days left anymore. It won't be long before winter sets in and then it's too late!

# Chapter 20
# The Elevator Crash

Dorothy McGuin and Millie Lyons are both leaving their apartments simultaneously and headed for the elevator, meeting up with Don Murke, Dan Blythe and Joe Kendall. They are all going to Bingo and Millie is the Bingo caller. Millie said, as they got in the elevator, "I'd better talk loud and clear, so I can be heard by everybody." Dorothy said "You'll do fine, Millie. I'm sure. Your voice is good and loud and it carries." They continued their conversation as Dan pushed the lobby button on the panel and the elevator very slowly started to go down. Fear gripped the five tenants as they looked at each other questioningly as if to say, "What's happening? What's wrong? Why is the elevator going so slow?" All of a sudden, they heard a snap and then a deafening sound and the elevator started a fast drop with everybody screaming and crying as the floor opened up. It was hanging side ways with several of the tenants clinging to the edge of the floor, their bodies dangling in mid-air and a black bottomless pit below them, the elevator continued on down, breaking boards in the process, as the tenants lost their grip and plunged to the basement floor and their death. Clouds of dust, ashes, boards and smoke coated the five broken and maimed bodies, as they lay in a heap amidst the debris. Their mangled bodies twisted under piles of boards and metal cast a pall of death as they lay.

It was quiet, too quiet, as the faint crack of a board dropping on a motionless body, already fatally crushed by splinters of steel.

A moaning, groaning sound breaks the dead of silence as a foul stench permeates the air drifting upward. The repugnant odor is the result of dismembered bodies scattered haphazardly on the basement floor. Also, volumes of blood are seeping into the cracked cement adding to the stagnant smell in the air. It's as if someone threw each body part down, one by one, counting them for their own sickening pleasure.

Who could've done such a dastardly deed? What behooved someone to act in this manner?

The tenants were all seated in anticipation of the start of the game. Someone mentioned, "We are missing the Bingo caller, Millie and her friend Dorothy and Dan Blythe, Don Murke and Joe Kendall because they have been coming all the time. I don't think they've missed a game yet. Marcus happened to be there tonight because of the overtime he put in on Sunday, so he said, "Go ahead and start the game with a different caller and I'll check it out?" He left and came back in a few minutes with reddened eyes, a pale, sick look on his face, and he was hardly able to talk. He motioned for everyone to follow him, as he led them to what was once the elevator, now a large, gaping, black hole housing the bodies of Millie, Dorothy, Don, Dan and Joe. The tenants started screaming, crying and flailing their arms, not knowing what else to do. Jack White said, "Call the police. This act of violence has got to be reported. What sort of sick person is infiltrating the apartment complex again? How many people are down there and who are they?" Jack wanted to know.

Marcus said, "We won't know until after the police department gets down to the basement floor and checks everything out. I hear the police coming right now.

Police Chief, Charles, was the first to approach what was once the elevator, followed by a string of policemen and detectives with investigative devices. The policemen made arrangements to ascend into the mammoth manhole to retrieve the bodies and body parts. The odor is unbearable as the policemen wear masks to help eliminate some of the smell. When they reached the basement floor, the shock was unbelievable. A policeman gave the following report. "Joe's head was dismembered from the rest of his body, as it rolled against the side of the basement wall. His eyes bulging out of their sockets in a fixed stare. Millie's head is intact, but her legs are scattered on the basement floor. Dorothy's head was detached part way, and it is bleeding profusely. It was still attached by some muscle and tissue. Dan's body is intact, but various bone, are sticking through his skin, his nose is missing and his eyes are gouged out. Don is detached at the waist, and his upper torso got thrown to the farther end of the basement floor, while his lower torso is lying against a side wall. All have the markings of a gruesome death, inflicted at the hands of a sick serial killer. To further complicate the investigation, hoards of insects and a snake, have infested the body of the deceased. In a corner a large rat is gnawing on Joe's neck which is detached from his body, while another huge rat has chewed off both of Millie's feet. The snake is draped over Dorothy's head, absorbing the blood from her body.

The stench was getting so bad Police Chief, Charles, called up for some face masks, which were dropped down the hole. A pulley was constructed to hoist body parts off of the basement floor. After all the bodies and body parts were identified, they were transported to Brown's Mortuary for final preparations, church services and burial.

An emergency meeting was held in the recreation parlor this evening at 7:00 PM to get a list of the victims that were killed in the elevator crash. Jack White said, "The people were Millie Lyons, Dorothy McGuin, Don Murck, Dan Blythe, and Joe Kendall. They were all victims of a serial killer, running rampant since 1995 in the apartment complex.

Past history revealed Millie Lyons and her husband, Don, moved into the complex four years ago. Don is retired from the railroad and Millie is retired from a secretarial position she held for forty years. Don has been in poor health for years due to his heart. They have two daughters Maria and Shelly. Maria lives in Bixby with one child and her husband, Bob, and Shelly live in East St. Louis, Missouri with two children and her husband, George.

Dorothy McGuin, 84 has been living at the complex for five years, never been married and retired from her teaching job at Rockwood High School for thirty five years. The last ten years were spent as the principal of Rockwood High School.

Don Murke, 70, has been living at the complex for seven years. Don is divorced and the father of one daughter, Gloria, who lives at Blumesville with her husband Dick and son. Don was in the retail men's clothing business, owning the Men's Clothing store for thirty two years in downtown Rockwood, Illinois.

Joe Kendall, 74, is retired from the hardware business of forty seven years. He owned and operated Joe's Hardware store on the south end of downtown Rockwood. Joe's wife Karen passed away four years ago and he has four children, two boys and two girls. Bob is married and living at St. Louis, Missouri with his wife Mary, and two children. Carl is living at Plattsville, Illinois with four girls and his wife Beth. Phyllis is married and livings at Morrow, Mississippi with husband Nick and their six children. Joan is married and living at Landsville, New York with her five children and her husband Sam.

Dan Blythe, 72, is the owner of Dan's Diner. His wife passed away, leaving three children. His daughter Anna is married to husband Jack with two children, living in Hicksville, Missouri. His son, Charles is married to wife Mary, with six children, also living in Hicksville, Missouri. His son, Jason is married to wife Paula, with four kids and they live in Biloxi, Mississippi.

All the victims' families have been notified, expressed remorse and grief that their loved one's life came to such an abrupt and bitter end at the hands of a serial killer in the elevator shaft several hundred feet below. Now, a mammoth gaping, hole with plumes of dust still seeping upward to fill the whole complex with a foul stench that permeates all the floors. The elevator hole has been cleaned up, the bodies have been removed and the police are doing a door to door investigation, as to any leads or sightings.

All the tenants must disclose their whereabouts at the time of the elevator crash. Some of them were in the recreation parlor waiting for the bingo game to start, while still others were in their apartment, not even attending the Bingo game. Some took a taxi to LaBamba's Restaurant for supper. By the time they got to Sue and Jane's apartment, they didn't bother to come in and sit down, but remained standing at the door questioning them, "Have you seen any unusual activity at the complex the day the elevator crashed?" They both replied, "No, not at all." The policeman asked, "Where were both of you at the time the elevator crashed?" Sue replied, "I was watching television and my mother, Jane, was taking her daily walk. Why do you want to know, officer? Is there something wrong?" Officer Jones replied, "Just checking ma'am. Were asking everybody. Mostly a routine check. Nothing to get alarmed about, just standard police procedure."

The next day the policemen were lowered into the black hole again for further investigation before they finally closed the hole up permanently. The bodies had been recovered hoisted up and transferred to Brown Mortuary for further observation and preparation. There were no fingerprints around the elevator, because there were layers of dust everywhere.

A new elevator will be installed within the week, so the tenants need to continue to take the back stairs, until the elevator has been completed.

Marcus made an announcement last night at the complex at a 7:00 PM meeting that services are being held at 7:00 PM this Wednesday at Rockwood Community Church in honor of the five tenants that lost their lives in the elevator crash. Services are pending otherwise for further investigation."

Pastor Hale was amazed at the well attendance of people that congregated for the service from the complex and otherwise. People were standing against the walls and in the back of the church with chairs being brought in to accommodate the elderly. Pastor Hale's sermon was befitting for the occasion, as it was focused on the after life as it is likened to our life here on earth. People were also sitting on chairs outside the church, to almost across the street, as extra speakers were set up, so Pastor Hale's sermon could be heard outside. The families of the victims could be seen in the church and some seated outside. Psalms were sung as the collection basket was passed around. Dismissal was given by Pastor Hale and a reminder to be back next Wednesday night for services again. Everybody filed out, while the complex group headed for the LaBamba Restaurant in downtown Rockwood, and others went home. A round table discussion was held with Marcus conducting. After about an hour everybody left for the complex and their apartment. A slow, steady rain was beginning to start, spreading a chill and a need for a jacket, on an early October evening. As Marcus was saying, "Given a few more weeks it will be colder than this. None of us will be going out much anymore in the evenings because of the weather and the danger." Several women tenants said, "We're not as scared as you guys. If we want to go we'll go, right ladies?" and they remarked, "That's right. We're not going to sit in our apartment for the rest of our lives because of some crazy nut running around killing people. We know how to be careful. What do you think we are, Marcus, stupid?"

Marcus said, "That isn't what I meant exactly. What I really meant was, if you and your lady friends are planning on going out for the evening after dark; please make sure you have transportation to and from your destination. When you return, also make sure you have your key and your card to get back into the complex. We don't know what will happen to Dan's Diner since it is closed now and you couldn't make any telephone calls from over there. So, just be careful. I don't want to see anything happen to anybody anymore. Too much has happened already."

Someone then asked Marcus, "In light of all that's happened, Marcus, do you think the complex will be condemned or just closed up, and we'd all have to find another place to live?" Marcus said, "I don't know what will happen. I have no idea at this point I don't know anymore than you do."

A couple of the tenants expressed interest in moving out of the complex because of all the deaths that have occurred since Fern Taylor's death in 1995. Dale said, "This last killing took five at one time. We live in a state of constant fear from the time we get up in the morning until we go to bed at night. You never know what's going to happen. We're plain scared. In fact, all three of us went yesterday to check another complex out and we decided to move in there at the beginning of next month."

Dale, Simon and I will miss all of you, but remember; you're all welcome to come over anytime to visit. Call before you come to make sure we're home.

As this conversation came to a close, they were all standing under the awning at LaBamba's Restaurant, waiting for the rain to subside. Then they got into their cars and taxi's and went their own way.

## Rockwood vs. Bixby College

Since Marcus got a reduction in his deputizing hours he has more free time to spend at the complex in the evenings, either playing cards, watching television or going on an evening outing by bus with tenants from the complex. Marcus made arrangements with the bus driver to take a group from the complex to the football game which they all wanted to see between Rockwood and their rival team of Bixby. They all went and sat as a group enjoying the game and refreshments. The game ended with Rockwood beating Bixby 24-7. Everybody boarded the bus and headed back to the apartment complex, with Marcus getting in his car and driving back to the apartment.

When Marcus came home he knew it would be too late to call the Plattsville Women's Prison, so he decided to wait until the next day. He wasn't hungry for a snack either because he had pie and coffee at LaBamba's Restaurant, so he went straight to bed.

Jacob, Dale and Simon have already moved to the Brinkson Apartments, about five blocks south of the Rockwood Apartment Complex. They all agreed this is a good move, at least there is nothing going on at the Brinkson Apartments like at the Rockwood Apartment Complex. Some of the apartment complex tenants went to visit Dale, Simon and Jacob and were very impressed with the apartments and their surroundings. The main reason they were immensely impressed was because the Brinkson Apartments didn't have the shadow of death hanging over them. Tenants at the Rockwood Apartments are getting an eerie feeling as they enter the lobby from the outside. This feeling stays with us until we leave the complex. Upon our return it's the same story. George, Louis and Arnold are considering making the move to the Brinkson Apartments because of everything that has transpired at the apartment complex. The prices of the apartments are the same as what we are paying now. George Brown, Lewis Lode and Arnold Blare went down to the office on the lobby floor and made a payment and the arrangements to move in by November 1, 2002, which would be in one week.

George, Lewis and Arnold said goodbye to all of their friends here at the apartment complex, in hopes of seeing them soon under different circumstances. They moved into their new apartments immediately.

Arnold said, "We are very happy and pleased with our new accommodations and our privileges are the same. Our activities are a full agenda of birthday parties, meetings, dances, national holiday parties, bingo, church service and so forth. We also have a key and a card to enter and exit the complex and we come and go as we please."

Many of the tenants of both complexes frequent Bob's Diner, which used to be Dan's Diner, until Dan Blyth became a victim of circumstances at the elevator crash that killed five people. They also meet at LaBamba's Restaurant in downtown Rockwood for meetings and luncheons.

## The Pit Bull's Gone Again…

Marcus was relaxing in his apartment last night in front of the television, when an "All Points Bulletin" was issued by the Rockwood Police Department. It was in regards to someone opening the gate and releasing six dogs which were out in a dog run for exercise, among them the pit bull that mauled the Police Chief's mother, Jean Blane, to death in the elevator at the Rockwood Apartment Complex. The pit bull was the only evidence the police had in the case, and now he was gone again, for the second time.

Marcus called the police station immediately and asked them if he needed to come and help and they said, "Yes, we need your help. Come down as soon as you can, because we're short handed and having a heck of a time getting help tonight. Some crazy fool came by and opened the gate and let the six dogs out and we'll have to contact the dog catcher tonight and see if he can find them. Hopefully there all running in a pack somewhere, so they can be easily spotted. I'll see you in a little bit. Goodbye."

Marcus put on his jacket and badge and left for the police station. When he arrived policemen were standing outside talking and the whole station was lit up. They were waiting for the dog catcher and his assistant, to brief them on this search. Marcus will be riding in the police car with another policeman in search of the dogs. He will be in contact by car phone with other policemen, as they continue their search for the dogs, especially the pit bull. The policemen are canvassing the whole city, the sidewalks, alleys, parks, anywhere a pack of dogs might congregate. As they were driving they heard a howling sound and they followed the lead, but it turned out to be a dead end. They headed out of town in hopes of seeing a pack of dogs along the highway, but that didn't happen. At this point, they will have to solicit the help of the public. If anybody had seen the dogs they are to call the police department.

# CHAPTER 21
# FUNERAL AT THE GYM

The bodies and body parts are being stored for several days at the Brown Mortuary because of the on going investigation into the deaths of five tenants at the Rockwood Apartment Complex. Detectives have been brought in from the St. Louis, Missouri area to assist in the investigation of the elevator crash and the five deaths involved. So far nothing has turned up. It seems like it has come to a standstill.

Several Days Later...

Rockwood High School is making preparations for the five tenants that died in the elevator crash at the Rockwood Apartment Complex. The students are setting up chairs in the gym for a memorial service tomorrow morning and burial to follow at the Rockwood Cemetery. A large luncheon will follow at the Rockwood High School cafeteria.

Flowers are being delivered all day long and set up accordingly.

The Next Morning...

Flowers are still being delivered this morning, as the five, closed caskets are being wheeled down the aisle. They are placed towards the front in a semi-circle, so each one can be seen. Three of the caskets are bronze and the two women's caskets are light blue, with a large spray of flowers on top of each of the five caskets. Pastor Hale of the Rockwood Community Church conducted the service with beautiful psalms to our Lord, and a sermon commemorating as he said, "The five people that gave their lives in the elevator, so that others might live." The victim's families and relatives sat in mourner's row and during the sermon there wasn't a dry eye in the gym. For some it was more than just a dry eye, it was loud weeping and words were spoken. Some more prayers followed by Pastor Hale and a response from the congregation. At the close of the memorial service Pastor Hale asked, "Will one member of each victim's family come forward and take one flower from the spray on the casket and place it on the gravesite after the grave has been closed? Thank you."

This was conducted in a mannerly order again, with tears flowing freely. Every chair in the gym was taken up, the bleachers were full and chairs were set up outside of the gym, namely, in the hallway and they were full, so many people had to stand at the entrance to the high school. There were speakers set up outside of the high school, for those that couldn't get in.

Everybody went to their cars to drive to their final resting place in Rockwood Cemetery. They were all buried in the cemetery, some beside their spouses and Dorothy, that never married, was buried beside her mother and father. Dan was divorced and he was buried beside his mother and father also.

Pastor Hale said a few prayers again and dismissed everybody saying, "A free lunch will be served in the Rockwood High School Gym. Please feel free to come. Thank you." Everybody immediately ascended on the gym for a free lunch and some light conversation, maybe meeting a friend or two they hadn't seen in a long time. The tenants from the Rockwood Apartment Complex joined the throng of people that were lined up for the lunch. Lunch consisted of meat sandwiches, potato chips, potato salad, cole slaw, pop, coffee, cookies and cake. There wasn't enough room in the cafeteria for everybody to eat at one time, so one group ate while the others waited, till everybody had eaten. After the luncheon and conversation goodbyes were said and everybody left. A light lusting of snow is beginning to fall, as it is November 15, 2002.

## Nursing Home...

Don, Millie Lyon's husband, was transferred to the Rockwood Nursing Home after the initial shock and the funeral had wore off, he was worse than ever. When he received the news about Millie's death he was totally devastated. His family had to take him to the Rockwood Hospital that night for an injection and an overnight stay for observation, because of his heart. He still keeps repeating all day long to himself, "My Millie, my Millie, what happened to her? Why doesn't she come home to me? Where is she? I'm so lost without her. Please bring her back to me." No one can console him and there's no one to take care of him either, so his daughter decided to put him in the Rockwood Nursing Home where he would get his meals and better care. Don didn't seem to mind, but he still misses Millie and wants her back. The residents are beginning to dwindle down because of the danger of living there. The fear of death clings to them all day and night, to the point of making them sick. Several of the tenants are complaining about headaches, stomach pain, and a bad case of nerves and various other symptoms that could be related to worry, anxiety, and fear of the unknown. Bob said, "I was so upset after that elevator crash with five people dead, I vomited half the night from fear. My wife, Judy, didn't know what to do. We are also, at the present, thinking abut moving out of here. This is terrible. How does the management expect us to live under these conditions? I don't see them living here! I wish they would lock this place up! It would suit me just fine."

As of now, there are about forty tenants left, without Dan, Bob and Judy leaving. If things continue in this fashion, the apartment complex runs the risk of getting locked up. It might be just a matter of time.

Paul and Clara Short are also thinking about moving into the Brinkson apartment complex, five blocks south of the Rockwood Apartment Complex. They visited Jacob, Simon and Dale and were very impressed by what they saw and heard from Dale, and his friends. Paul made the

*BLOOD SUCKING SERIES NO. 1: THE FINAL FLOOR*

remark, "We could live over here for the same amount of money and not have to deal with the thought of murder everyday." Clara agreed saying, "I told Paul, I'm just plain scared in this place and I want to get out of here. We're going to pay our first months rent tomorrow and we're moving next week. We hate to leave all of you, but it's just too dangerous here. Twelve people dead in seven years. Think about it. I wish you would all move for your own sake. You might be sorry if you don't. Maybe then they'd be forced to lock this place up. Paul, we'd better go upstairs and start packing now. We were going to start tonight, remember?" Paul said, "Yes, I remember," and they left.

Sue and Jane have still decided to stay as Sue says, "Because we think all of the murders will be solved eventually. Something will happen and it will tie that happening into the other twelve murders. Just wait and see. Jane agreed saying, "I think Sue is correct. Something will happen and it will all be out in the open. We are not planning on moving, and if we wind up the only two people living in here, then that's the way it's going to be, I guess."

Another Meeting…

Marcus posted another note on the bulletin board for a meeting instead of a card game, because the meeting was more important.

Everybody in the complex came to the meeting, because they all knew it was important. When they arrived Tuesday night at 7:00 PM, Marcus got straight to the point by asking, "How many of you residents are planning to move out of this complex? Please be truthful." A lot of residents raised their hands, about half that were there. Marcus asked, "Paul and Clara Short, why do you want to leave?" They explained, "Because of the fear of what's been happening here for the past seven years." Marcus asked everybody, one by one, and they all gave the same answer. He said, "Those of you that are thinking about leaving, would you reconsider if we put more police and security guards around this place, to make it more livable?" They all shook their heads and said, "No!" Marcus asked them, "Would you reconsider if your rent was reduced considerably?" They all said, "No!" He then asked them this question, "Would you reconsider if your rent was cut in half?" They still said, "No!" Then Marcus said, "Okay, that's all I want to know. I'm sorry we couldn't accomplish anything here this evening. You all have your own free will from God to do what you want. I won't stand in your way. No hard feelings. It was nice having you as long as we did. If any of you have a refund coming from the office, please check before you leave. Thank you!" The meeting is adjourned and you're all free to leave. Everybody that is planning to move out of the apartment complex got up and left and the residents that are going to continue to stay lagged behind, including Sue and her mother, Jane and some of the others.

Sue and Jane still vowed they are staying as did some of the other residents. Marcus said, "Good, because I am even considering moving into the apartment complex because the landlord raised my rent." The Rockwood apartment Complex is for retired people, but Sue lives there with her mother and she's still working, so there's no reason why they wouldn't let Marcus move in. They do make exceptions, you know.

Marcus checked the apartment situation out the next day and everything was fine. He paid his rent and will move in this weekend. He might as well move in because he's there all the time anyway. Marcus couldn't afford to pay more rent than what he is paying now. The only difference is he had a garage at the other apartment and at the Rockwood Apartment Complex there aren't any garages. Your car is outside all the time, even in inclement weather. That's something he has to put up with from now on.

The Weekend's Here...

Marcus started moving into his apartment early Saturday afternoon, right next to Sue and Jane. They helped him unload his belongings while he went and got one load after the next. After six loads he was finally through. At dinner time Jane prepared something for them to eat and they continued to unload Marcus' things until after midnight. Then Sue and Jane went back to their apartment and Marcus went on to bed.

The next morning they continued to help him until they had everything in place, and no clutter. In the evening they all went out for supper at the LaBamba Restaurant in downtown Rockwood, and then back home. Sue and Jane went to their apartment and Marcus went on to his to retire early, because he had to get up at 6:00 AM the next morning for work.

Well, on second thought, Marcus decided to call Betty at the Women's prison in Plattsville, Illinois to see how she's doing. He hadn't talked to her for quite awhile and she wasn't feeling good the last time he talked to her about six weeks ago. The phone rang about six times before Betty answered, "Hello." Marcus Said, "Hello, Betty. Why did it take you so long to answer?" Betty said, "I wasn't feeling good, Marcus. I was lying down for a little while. Marcus asked her, "Do you know what the pain in you stomach is coming from?" Betty said, "No, I don't. The doctors are still not through doing tests on me. I have to have some more tests done tomorrow. I've been starting to vomit from this pain; I'm worried about this whole thing, wouldn't you be, Marcus?" He replied, "Yes, Betty I suppose I'd be worried too. Is it something that you're eating maybe?" Betty answered, "No, I've abstained from different kinds of food and it doesn't seem to make any difference. Marcus said, "Betty, I don't think I told you what happened here at the complex or did you read it in the newspaper? About the elevator crash, that killed three men and two women, all of them on their way to play Bingo in the recreation parlor? It was awful. I discovered it when none of them showed up for Bingo. It left a huge, gaping hole in the floor. The police don't know who did it, but someone cut the cable on the elevator and that caused the elevator to drop into a black bottomless pit." Betty said, "I saw a picture of it in our prison paper and I was shocked. I wonder who would have the nerve to do such an abominable thing." Marcus said, "About half of the people are moving out of the complex, five blocks south to the Brinkson's Apartment Complex. We had a meeting and none of those tenants want to stay anymore, so half are leaving. So far, the rest are staying. In fact, my landlord raised the rent on me, and I moved out last Saturday. I moved into one of the vacated apartments in the Rockwood Apartment Complex.

Oh, I forgot to tell you, Betty. Remember, that pit bull that mauled the police chief's mother to death? Well, the pit bull and five other dogs were released by an unknown person, on purpose, to run through the streets of Rockwood undetected. The pit bull is the only evidence we have in the death of the Police Chief, Charles, mother Jean Blane. The dogs have not been found as of yet." Betty answered, "Sounds like you have a lot going on in Rockwood, Marcus. In prison, it's the same thing, day in and day out. We don't have any contact with the outside world, unless the paper or television. I'm so glad when I get out of here. I counted 172 days left today, not quite six months yet. Time goes by so slow, especially when you're counting the days."

Marcus asked her, "Betty, are you planning on coming back to Rockwood?"

Betty said, "Yes," because her parents are there and she wouldn't know where else to go.

Marcus said, "Betty, I guess I'd better hang up now and get to bed, so I'll be able to get up at 6:00 AM tomorrow morning. I'll be calling again to checkup on those tests. Goodbye!"

Betty said, "Goodbye, Marcus."

Marcus went to bed as soon as he got off the phone and lay there thinking to himself, "What's wrong with Betty? Why is she so sick? She was never sick like this before, never. I don't understand this. Did something happen to her?"

Marcus went to sleep with those thoughts on his mind, only to be awakened at 3:00 AM by Betty's father, Dave, telling him, "Marcus, Betty got violently ill later on in the evening after you and Betty hung up and she has been transferred to the prison hospital where she is in intensive care and very ill. He said, "Betty's mother, Martha, is very worried and wants to make the trip to Plattsville, Illinois to see Betty. Marcus, the reason I called was to tell you about Betty and ask you if you wanted to come along." Marcus listened intently and said, "Yes, I'd like to come along. I have two weeks vacation coming, so I'll talk to my boss in the morning and call you back. I'll call as soon as I find out this morning. Will you be home, Dave?" Dave said, "Yes, we'll be home waiting for your call. Goodnight." Marcus said "Goodnight," and hung up the receiver.

Morning came all too early and Marcus arose, got ready, ate and left for work. He contacted his boss and told him about Betty and his boss said he could start his two week vacation anytime he wanted. Marcus started his vacation immediately and left the college to go to his apartment and call Dave. When Dave answered Marcus told him, "I can start my vacation today and I am free to leave anytime your ready." Dave said, "We're ready anytime you are Marcus because we're already packed." Marcus said, "I have to pack my suitcase and then I'll be over to pick you up. We can go in my car, because I'm more familiar with it on the highway." They both hung up.

When Marcus, Dave and Martha started on the highway it was 1:30 PM. It was a sixteen hour drive, so by the time it got dark they would be checking into a motel somewhere along the road. They drove as far as Larksville, Illinois just before you cross into Indiana, and spent the night at the Larksville Motel. The next morning after a good breakfast, they started driving again only to encounter road construction and one lane traffic for several miles. But they kept pushing on. They reached Plattsville, Illinois about 5 o'clock that evening. Plattsville's population is 45,452 people and is surrounded by the Hawk River. The women's prison is located about five miles south of the city in an open field area. A large buff colored brick building with additional buildings connected to it. Marcus pulled up in the parking lot; they got out and walked into the main entrance to the desk attendant. They introduced themselves and explained what they were there for and whom they wanted to see and they were immediately escorted down a long corridor into a darkened private room with a strange, stale odor.

Dave and Martha went to her bedside first and Dave said, "Betty, We're Dave and Martha, your mother and father, and here is your friend Marcus. C'mere, son, and talk to Betty. Tell her who you are." Marcus came forward and said, "Hello, Betty. I'm Marcus, Your friend. How are you? We thought we'd come up and see you, because none of us have been here before. We didn't have any problems finding our way up here."

Betty winced as if she was in pain and could barely speak above a whisper. Her eyes were closed half of the time and she seemed very sick. Marcus asked her, "Betty, do you know who we are?" And she said, "MMMom, Dad and Marcus. Someone, please help me. I'm so terribly sick." Marcus went up to the front desk and explained the situation and they sent a nurse back with a shot of morphine for the pain. While Marcus and her parents were there, they were asked to meet with Dr. Miller in his office for consultation. They immediately went in and sat down as Dr. Miller came in and told them Betty has inoperable stomach cancer. It's impossible to operate on this type of cancer because it has progressed and attacked her other vital organs. Martha began weeping uncontrollably as Dave asked the forbidding question, "Doctor, how much time does Betty have left? We'd like to know." Dr. Miller said, "About three or four weeks at the most. Please make the most of the time you'll be spending with her. Thank you.

# Chapter 22
# The Capture

Late one night, about two weeks ago, while Marcus was sound asleep, he received a call from Betty's dad, Dave. Dave said to him, "Marcus, Betty passed away in her sleep about an hour ago. I'm sorry to have to call you during the night with such bad news, but I knew you'd be interested in finding out. They said the body will be shipped to Rockwood tomorrow afternoon and they would be notifying the Brown Mortuary. The mortuary will set up a viewing date and Pastor Hale will conduct the funeral service at the mortuary." Marcus said, "I'm sorry to hear about Betty's passing Dave, and give my condolences to your wife, Martha. I know she was very sick when we were at the prison hospital that day."

The next day Betty's body was shipped to the Brown Mortuary for the final preparations. Private viewing time would be the next day at 1:00 PM for Dave, Martha, Marcus and a few other relatives. An article will be in the Rockwood Flyer obituary tomorrow morning. The room was full to capacity for the evening viewing. Betty had a green dress on and her dark hair was neatly coiffed. The next morning at 10:00 AM Pastor Hale conducted a funeral service at the Brown Mortuary with full attendance. Burial followed the service at Rockwood cemetery, clouded by a haze of snow and sleet and sub zero temperature.

After the burial Pastor Hale announced there would be a luncheon in the Rockwood Community Church basement for all that would like to attend. A lot of people attended the luncheon and visited with Dave, Martha and Marcus at length. After that everyone went home.

In the weeks that followed, Marcus visits Betty's grave often, since now a headstone has been erected and a name, dates and words etched in stone.

Christmas and New Years Day have come and gone, and January is around the corner. A long, cold, dark and dreary month. Marcus posted the monthly meeting on the bulletin board in the main lobby for tomorrow night at 7:00 PM, urging everyone to attend in the recreation parlor. The next night at 6:30 PM all the residents started filing in and took their seats except Sue and Jane. Well, someone said "there just late." Marcus said, "We'll start the meeting and they can always come in and take a seat."

In the meantime Sue told her mother Jane she was ready to go to the meeting, "Are you ready mother?" Jane said, "No, not quite. I'll be down in a little bit." Sue left and got into the elevator. In an instant, the other side of the elevator opened up and the strangest person walked in. You couldn't differentiate between a man or woman, with a long coat, sloppy trousers, old boots, a hat and glasses and long disheveled hair and a pungent, filthy odor. Unrecognizable in the face because of a mask they said, "Hand over your money or I'll kill all of you." Sue thought the voice sounded sort of familiar. All of a sudden the elevator stopped between two floors, made a jerking and shaking noise as the assailant lost control of his revolver and it dropped to the floor. Sue hurriedly picked it up and directed it at the strange character and said, "Either you pull your mask down or I'll pull it down for you. You have your choice." They immediately pulled their mask down and it was Jane, Sue's own mother. Can you believe this? Sue screamed "Mother! I can't believe that's really you! What are you doing all dressed up like this?" Jane said, "Oh, I just did it for a joke and I didn't mean any harm. I pretended like I was the assailant. What a laugh!"

Sue said, "No mother, it's not a laugh! You are the killer! Mother you've been the killer all along, ever since Fern Taylor's death in 1995,

## BLOOD SUCKING SERIES NO. 1: THE FINAL FLOOR

Mr. Cain's snake bite, Mr. Sloan's gunshot murder, the pit bull murder, the gassing of three people and the cutting of the elevator cable that made it crash to the basement floor killing 5 people. Mother, how could you kill all twelve of those people? And this evening you were going to rob me and then kill me. Mother, how could you rob and kill your only child?"

"Mother, no wonder you were never around right at the time a murder happened. It just seemed strange that you were always gone." Jane said, "Sue, I'm sorry I killed all those people, because it must be a sickness with me. I don't know why I do it. I remember a long, long time ago, I killed three people and I don't know why I did that to this day. I guess I'm sicker than I really know."

Sue was still crying as she said, "I'm going to do one of the hardest things I've ever done in my entire life and that is to call the police on my own mother. I never thought I'd ever have to do anything like that, but it looks like I do."

Sue called the Rockwood Police Department, with Police Chief, Charles, answering and explained the whole story to him. Charles was shocked as he could be saying, "You mean we actually have the killer in our midst, after all those years, Sue? I believe you, of course, but its hard for me to comprehend that it's your own mother, Jane. I would've never guessed it was her in a million years. Sue, didn't you have any idea that it could've possibly been her?"

Sue answered, "No, Charles, not really. Although I thought it kind of strange and odd that she was never around when a murder took place, she was always conveniently gone from the apartment around that time."

Charles said, "Well, Sue, I guess there's nothing left to say. I'm truly sorry that it was your mother that committed these twelve murders, because she doesn't look like the type. I guess nowadays you don't have to look like the type either; you just have to play the part. Correct?" Sue said, "That's right, Charles."

Charles said, "I'll go over to the apartment complex with several other policemen, and apprehend her, and bring her back to the police station for questioning and book her into jail. She'll have to stay in jail now until her trial and sentencing. I'm sorry, Sue, but she can't be released into your custody anymore." Sue said, "I figured that. Maybe it's just as well. At this point, I can hardly stand to be around my own mother, for what she did to those people. It just makes me sick. I'm so devastated."

Charles said, "Our prayers for the last couple of years at the Rockwood Community Church have finally been answered. It always helps to pray. I'll be talking to you later, Sue. Bye!" Sue said, "Bye."

Charles and several other policemen pulled up in front of the apartment complex, went inside, and found Jane sitting in the lobby waiting for the police. Several reporters from the Rockwood Flyer were interviewing her and taking her photograph. Looking at Jane Linton, 74, sitting on a divan in the lobby of the Rockwood Apartment Complex, one would never guess that she is a serial killer. Jane is a quiet, demure, soft spoken woman with, actually, very little to say. It's still hard for most people to believe that Jane Linton is the serial killer. Police Chief, Charles, asked her identity and a few other questions, handcuffed her, and took her to the police station for further questioning. Jane was assigned a private cell, no. 21, being put in immediately, only to be brought out later for questioning.

Jane was brought out of her cell to answer a barrage of questions several hours later. Charles asked her, "How was it that you never got caught in any of the murders, or apprehended from a resident at the complex? How did you get by with everything?"

Jane said, "I watched my time very closely, when the residents were all in the recreation parlor for a meeting or something. I also made sure, checking periodically, to see if there was anybody else around before I did my dastardly deed. I always made sure the coast was clear before I proceeded on. I also worked very, very, fast, never encountering anybody."

Charles asked her, "Jane, weren't you ever worried about getting caught red handed?" Jane said, "No, not really, because I knew about what time all the residents were in their apartments. I had that all figured out. I was pretty shrewd."

Charles asked her again, "Jane, given all that has happened in these last eight years, since Fern Taylor's death in 1995, if you would've known everything then like you do now, would you have still continued on with your evil intentions?"

Jane said, "Maybe and maybe not. That's a hard question to answer. It would've all depended on how my mind was working at the time. I haven't' been on medication for a very long time and that diminished the working power in my brain, or reducing it to a cluster of bundled up nerves.

Charles continued, "Jane, I'm sure you realized at the beginning of this question and answer session that you were hooked up to a lie detector machine and so far, everything you have told us has been true, or else the machine would've caught it. Thank you! I appreciate that."

Jane, for the remainder of the time you are incarcerated here you will be confined to cell No. 21 and you will be outside once a day for exercise about an hour and then back into your cell. I have no idea how long you'll be here because that depends on the court in St. Louis, Missouri where you will be tried, probably a couple of months from now. Whatever the judge in St. Louis, Missouri decides for your sentencing, you'll have to abide with that."

Jane said, "I realized the wrong I've done and sometimes wish I could undo it, but I know I can't. It's too late for that. I just have to go on from here as best I can." And with that statement, she proceeded into cell No. 21.

## Sue Comes to Visit...

Sue came to visit the next day and Jane was happy to see her. Sue and Jane were both reduced to tears at the prospect of not being able to see each other over the next months, because of the fact that Sue doesn't have a car to go see Jane where she will be in prison. The only way Sue can see Jane is by bus or if she gets a ride with somebody that's willing to take her.

Sue and Jane discussed the murders at length, which made Jane even more uneasy and Sue angry and upset. By the time Sue left for the apartment complex, she and Jane were not on speaking terms again. So, as usual, she left early and walked back to the apartment complex.

When she got back, Marcus came over and she invited him into the apartment and he said, "Sue, I'm sorry about your mother being involved in those twelve killings. It must be real hard on you at this time. What's going to happen to her?"

Sue said, "Well, she'll only be here for now, and then she'll be transferred to St. Louis, Missouri to a prison there for a trial and sentencing. I won't be seeing her much anymore, I guess, because that's too far away and I don't drive. I wonder if I would be allowed to call her. Marcus kept listening to her and he finally said, "Maybe I can take you up to wherever she'll be." Sue said, "We'll have to see how things go."

Sue made coffee in the kitchen and gave a cup to Marcus accompanied by a piece of pie, which Marcus hurriedly devoured. He said, "Thank you," and went back to his own apartment. He watched the news, and they had the review for the whole day, even a re-enactment of everyone of the twelve murders committed by Jane. No, he didn't call Sue, because he figured she's going through enough as it is. Marcus is aware of the fact that the apartment complex residents are whispering behind Sue's back because of the murder Jane has committed at the complex. Pastor Hale said, "Sue isn't responsible for the sins of her mother, but Jane is." Marcus vowed he's going to talk to some of the residents that are guilty of these things, telling them not to ostracize Sue, nor snub her, but include Sue in different functions and make her feel welcome, just as if this had never happened.

Marcus was just ready to go to bed when the phone rang and it was Sue asking him, "Marcus, this is Sue. Are you in bed already? Marcus said, "No, not quite. Why? What's wrong?" Sue said, "The police department wants me to come down right now and they wouldn't say why. Can you take me down with the car?" Marcus said, "Of course, I'll be ready in a minute. Are you ready to go?"Sue said, "Yes, I'll meet you on the elevator." They each hung up and left their apartments.

They hurriedly rushed into the police station and were met by Charles, working late. Charles recounted this story: "One of the security guards patrolling the jail was walking past Jane's cell No. 21 and thought it was strange that he didn't see her, but all of a sudden in a corner he saw Jane's body dangling form the ceiling, with a bed sheet wrapped around her neck. He immediately called for help, and they lowered the body and took her to Rockwood hospital where they are treating her. Jane had tried to hang herself and needs 24 hour surveillance to make sure this doesn't happen again. She needs to stand trial for the twelve murders she committed. After this incident she might have to go to a larger facility like St. Louis where she can be monitored twenty four hours, day and night.

Sue and Marcus listened in silence and then went to the Rockwood Hospital to see Jane. She was in a private room awake when they walked in, crying because of what she tried to do. Jane said, "Oh, I'm so sorry, so sorry. I don't know what came over me. I guess I was so depressed and overcome with grief, I just decided to end it all. I'm sorry I chased you down here at this ungodly hour of the night. I can assure you it won't happen again. The hospital is going to medicate me for this mental problem I have." Marcus and Sue both said "We're glad your getting medicine for your mental problem." Sue said, "How long will you be in the hospital, mother?" Jane said, "They told me I would be in here about three or four days, and then Charles said, "You'll probably be moved to St. Louis, Missouri prison, closer to the trial." Jane made a remark, "I'll be glad when the trial is over, because I heard they can take quite awhile. I'm looking forward to it."

Sue and Marcus said it was getting late and they needed to leave and bid Jane goodnight. Jane said, "Goodnight, and thanks for coming out tonight. Please come back again as long as I'm here." Sue and Marcus said, "We'll be back before you leave, don't worry."

The next evening Sue and Marcus went to the Rockwood Hospital to visit Jane again. She said she would be leaving the hospital to go back to the police station the next day. Marcus and Sue stayed for about two hours and they left because Jane said she had to get to bed early because of her transfer to the police station the next day. After Marcus and Sue left, Jane lay in bed for a little while thinking. Then she got up, walked out into the hall where it was fairly dark, quiet, and no nurses or anyone else in sight and started walking down the hall. Suddenly, she came upon a room that said, "Medical Supplies" on the door. She entered the small room, turned on the light and saw a vast amount of bottled pills. Jane couldn't understand the medical terms on the bottle, but she took several bottles along anyway. When she got back to her room, she took three fourth's of a bottle of pills to end it all again and she lay on the bed waiting to die. Death didn't come, and she waited...waited...waited some more and still nothing happened. By this time, she felt awfully hot, the perspiration dripping off her face, as she started to get dizzy and feeling faint. A nurse making her nightly checks came into the room and noticed that something was amiss and started checking Jane. She noticed the medicine bottle with the pills that Jane had found was one-fourth full, so that means Jane consumed three fourths of a bottle of pills to take her life. The nurse reported this to the doctor on call and they immediately pumped her stomach. Among other contents in the stomach, a lot of pills were pumped out, and she was taken back to her private room, and put on surveillance watch for the remainder of the night.

The next morning she was transferred back to the police station, where she will be held until there is an opening for her at the St. Louis Prison in St. Louis, Missouri.

The Police Chief, Charles, reported to Sue and Marcus that she again tried to take her own life with a bottle of pills but she didn't succeed. Marcus and Sue were very upset, especially Sue. She was totally devastated. Sue told Charles to call her when her mother would be sent to St. Louis, Missouri. Within a few days Charles called back and said, "This is Police Chief, Charles, calling. Sue, your mother, Jane, is being released from jail tomorrow morning to be taken to St. Louis, Missouri. If you want to say goodbye to your mother, you'll have to come by this evening. Visiting hours are 6:00 PM-8:00 PM. Please abide by these rules."

That evening Sue and Marcus drove to the police station again and visited with Jane until visitation hours were over at 8:00 PM. Jane apologized to Sue for all the trouble she had caused through the years, and hoped she might see her during the trial or maybe a telephone call, if she was allowed. Sue nodded her head and thought that could be arranged. The next morning Jane was taken to St. Louis, Missouri Prison to stand trial for the murder of twelve people since 1995.

Jane in Prison...

Jane's been at the St. Louis Prison in St. Louis Missouri for several months now. Sue and Jane call each other back and forth and the news is always the same. Jane talks about the people that get life in prison, no chance for parole, another will be out in five years, and another person is in prison for life dealing drugs. Sue talks about the Rockwood Apartment Complex, Marcus, news about the people she used to know, a variety of things. Jane has a homesick tone to her voice asking about certain people.

We all know this could've been avoided, don't we? But it's too late now, read on.

A report was issued this morning that Jane's trial will start June 11, 2003 at 9:00 AM and last all week long or possibly longer. Sue and Marcus will stay the length of the trial and then go home. Sue will be on the witness stand testifying in regards to her mother, Jane, as best she's capable of. Marcus will not be called to the witness stand and he's glad of it.

This afternoon, Jane is outside with the other women prisoners for an hours worth of exercise which she doesn't do. It's a cool, spring day and Jane is wearing a jacket, leaning against the prison building, and deep in thought as to what will happen at the trial. Will she get life in prison, without parole, or will she get so many years in prison with a chance for parole? Time will tell. We don't know. What do you think? Or will she get off on good behavior? Let's find out!

# CHAPTER 23
# COURT

On Sunday, June 10, Marcus and Sue were on there way to the St. Louis, Missouri area to attend the trial of Jane Linton, Sue's mother, accused of killing twelve people at the Rockwood Apartment Complex in Rockwood Illinois. The trial will start tomorrow morning, Monday, June 11, 2003 at 9:00 AM in St. Louis, Missouri District Court. Not everyone is in attendance at this time. Only people that are related, a private friend or relative to the victim's families and the victim's families themselves. Also the family and private friends and relatives of Jane Linton.

Marcus called his brother, Adam, and asked him, "Can Sue and I stay at your house overnight while we are here, because during the day we will be in court." Adam said, "Sure, make yourself right at home. If you want anything, just holler. Marcus, your room is in the basement and Sue is upstairs. Actually, here is an extra house key for you, the length of time that you are here, just don't forget to return it." Marcus said, "Thank you, we won't forget to return it."

Marcus and Sue were sitting in the front room after supper visiting with Adam and his family. Since Sue is testifying as a witness, not much can be said about the case, until it's completely over. Just the bare necessities were mentioned.

*BLOOD SUCKING SERIES NO. 1: THE FINAL FLOOR*

Marcus retired at 10:00 PM and Sue sat up and got acquainted with Adam and his family some more. She went to bed at 11:30 PM, knowing she had to get up early the next morning. She was very tired from the long trip.

Marcus and Sue were up early the next morning, getting ready to go to court in downtown St. Louis. As they walked into the courtroom they could see it was practically standing room only. They found a place to sit down close to the front, as the judge started to review the case. Witness after witness testified as both attorneys questioned them at length. Mr. Slater was Jane's attorney and Mr. Snell was the victim's attorney. Mr. Cole was the presiding judge for the district court of St. Louis, Missouri. Twelve jury people were in their jury boxes.

Judge Cole announced, "The court will take a break and resume in fifteen minutes. This gives everybody a chance to regain their composure and collect their thoughts."

Judge Cole is back on the bench and ready to resume with the case. Sue is interrogated on the witness stand by Attorneys Slater and Snell as they field questions at her constantly. Questions such as, "Can you give us a brief description of your mother, Jane's past history of her mental breakdown, Sue?" Sue answered the attorney with this description, "Yes, I can. Mother was diagnosed with her mental illness years ago, when she killed three people in another state where we lived. She was in prison for awhile, and then she was released with medication to treat her mental condition."

Attorney Snell asked Sue, "What happened to bring your mother onto the killing scene again, Sue."

"My mother gradually started forgetting over the years to take her medication to control her desire to kill at random. If I remember correctly, the medication was very expensive, and that might've been one contributing factor that made her discontinue her medication." Attorney Snell asked her, "Sue, how old is your mother?" Sue said, "My mother is 74 years old." Attorney Snell said, "Thank you, you may step down." Sue stepped down and took her place beside Marcus towards the front.

The jury continued to listen intently at the descriptions by the witnesses and they studied each witness as they were interrogated by the attorneys. The jury studied the actions and composure of each witness, their fidgeting, nervous reaction to the point of stuttering, an indication that they're lying, a perspiring look on their face, having a hard time facing an attorney when being questioned and a variety of other facial expressions indicative of lying.

Fern Taylor's daughter, Rose, came from Seattle, Washington for the murder trial of her mother Fern Taylor. Rose was called to the witness stand to testify on her mother's behalf. Attorney Snell asked Rose, "Who do you think took your mother's life, Rose? Can you point to her?" Rose said, "I don't have to think who took my mother's life. I know for a fact who did." Rose lifted her hand and pointed at Jane. "There she is sitting in the front row, with a white blouse on and blue skirt. She's the serial killer, all right."

Attorney Snell said, "Rose, you may step down now. Thank you." Next witness is Ella Cain. Mrs. Cain walked up to the witness stand with her cane, barely hobbling along. Attorney Snell said, "Mrs. Cain, will you swear to tell the truth, the whole truth, and nothing but the truth, so help you God?" She said, "I will," and Attorney Snell proceeded on. "Mrs. Cain, Can you describe briefly what happened to Mr. Cain the night of his death?" Mrs. Cain said, "Of course, Bob went downstairs to get the mail and was bitten by a rattle snake in the elevator and was dead when they arrived at the hospital." Attorney Snell said, "Can you point to the person in this courtroom that you think killed your husband?" Mrs. Cain pointed to Jane and said, "There's the bitch. Lock her up again. That's all I have to say." Attorney Snell said, "Very well, Mrs. Cain, you may step down. Thank you!"

Next witness is Mary Sloan. Mrs. Sloan approached the witness stand and took her place. Attorney Slater asked her "Mary, will you swear to tell the truth, the whole truth, and nothing but the truth, so help you, God?" Mary said. "I will." She proceeded, "George and I were in the elevator, headed for the recreation parlor, when this unrecognizable person came out of nowhere, shot George in the head and ran off." Attorney Slater said, "Can you point to the person in the courtroom that killed your husband?" Mary said, "Yes, I can. It was Jane Linton, there in the front row. I can't stand to look at her ugly face."

Everybody in the apartment complex hates her for what she did. That was sickening! I hope she burns in hell for that!" Attorney Slater said, "You may step down from the witness stand. Thank you!"

Next witness coming up: Please be seated Ellen Gomey. Attorney Slater said, "Ellen, will you swear to tell the truth, the whole truth, and nothing but the truth, so help you God?" Ellen said, "I will." Attorney Slater said, "Ellen can you point out your mother's killer?" Ellen said, "I sure can. Right over there in the front row beside her attorney. Everyone knows she did it. It's common knowledge." Attorney Slater, "You may step down, Ellen. Thank you."

Next witness, please. Phyllis Jones is called to the witness stand. Attorney Slater asked her, "Phyllis, will you swear to tell the truth, the whole truth and nothing but the truth, so help you God." Phyllis replied, "I will." Attorney Slater asked her, "Phyllis, are you the daughter of Rich and Lila Burns?" Phyllis said, "Yes, I am and that dirty devil sitting in the front row murdered my mom and dad by asphyxiating them with gas. I could kill her with my bare hands if it were allowed." Attorney Slater said, "You may step down, Phyllis. Thank you."

Next witness please. Please be seated. Charles Blane, Chief of Police. Attorney Slater asked, "Charles, will you swear to tell the truth, the whole truth, and nothing but the truth, so help you, God?" Charles said, "I will." Attorney Slater asked, "Charles, who in this courtroom would you say is your mother's killer?" Charles pointed to Jane Linton and said, "That's her. That's the killer of my mother and the remainder of the eleven others that were killed. I'd like to shoot her myself, that's how mad I am. I hope she never gets out of prison."

Charles Blane was the last witness and Judge Cole dismissed court for the day. Everybody is to come back at 9:00 AM in the morning to resume the testifying. Marcus and Sue left district court and went back to Marcus' brother Adam and his family ate supper and retired early. Marcus and Sue sat on the front porch and visited for about an hour and Sue went upstairs to bed and Marcus continued to set outside for awhile and then he also went down to the basement and to bed.

The next morning everybody was up and raring to go. Marcus and Sue drove to the District Court, just as it started. Judge Cole said, "We are still continuing with the witnesses until we are done."

First witness for the day is Barbara Gorm. "Miss Gorm, will you step up to the witness stand, please." Attorney Slater said, "Barbara, will you raise your right hand? Do you swear to tell the truth, the whole truth and nothing but the truth, so help you, God?" Barbara said, "I will." Attorney Snell said, "I understand, Barbara, that you were Dorothy LaGuine's best friend?" Barbara said, "Yes, we were best friends for years." Attorney Snell said, "Barbara, do you have any idea who killed your best friend, Dorothy LaGuine?" Barbara said, "Most certainly, that older woman sitting beside the attorney. That's what I was told and I honestly believe that's the truth. What she did was horrible. I hope she gets her due punishment." Attorney Slater said, "You may step down from the witness stand, Barbara and thank you!"

Next witness, please. Shelly Byrd. Attorney Slater said, "Shelly, will you swear to tell the truth, the whole truth, and nothing but the truth, so help you, God?" Shelly said, "I do." Attorney Slater asked her, "Shelly, are you one of Millie Lyon's daughters?" Shelly said, "I am." Attorney Slater said, "Shelly, can you point out in the assembly today, the person or persons that you think is responsible for your mother's death?" Shelly said, "Yes, the lady in the front row with the white blouse and blue skirt." In a split second, Shelly jumped up and ran over to Jane, grabbed her by the throat and began to throttle her. Jane's face began to turn blue; she was gasping for air and making gurgling sounds in her throat. Immediately, two policemen pulled Shelly away from Jane as the courtroom was shocked into fear, not knowing what the outcome would be.

Shelly was cited for contempt of court by Judge Cole and he would deal with her later. Judge Cole said, "Everybody, please refrain from any outbursts of anger as you enter the witness stand. Thank you."

Next witness, please. Joan Mullen. Attorney Slater said, "Joan, will you swear to tell the truth, the whole truth and nothing but the truth,

*BLOOD SUCKING SERIES NO. 1: THE FINAL FLOOR*

so help you, God?" Joan said, "I do." Attorney Slater said, "Joan, are you one of Joe Kendall's daughters?" Joan said, "I am." Attorney Slater said, "Joan, can you point out to the court, which person killed your father, Joe Kendall?" Joan said, "I certainly won't hesitate one bit. The serial killer is sitting in the front row, with short, gray hair, a white blouse and blue skirt." Judge Cole said, "Thank you! You may step down, please."

Next witness, please. Gloria James. Attorney Snell said, "Gloria, will you swear to tell the truth, the whole truth and nothing but the truth, so help you, God?" Gloria said, "I do." Attorney Snell said, "Gloria, can you point out to the court, which person in here today killed your father?" Gloria jumped up in anger and pointed at Jane saying, "How could you do such a thing, cut the cable in the elevator, so the elevator crashed to the basement floor, killing five people? How could you?"

Judge Cole said, "Thank you! You may step down now and please return to your seat.

Next witness, please. Oliver Blythe. Attorney Snell said, "Oliver, are you Dan Blythe's son?" Oliver said, "Yes, I am."

"Oliver, will you swear to tell the truth, the whole truth, and nothing but the truth, so help your, God?" Oliver replied, I will." Attorney Snell said, "Very well then, Oliver. Can you pick out your father's killer here in district court today?" Oliver said, "I sure can and she knows it also. The woman in the front row, glaring up at all of us as if to say, I'm going to kill you all the next time I get the chance. "The Judge said, "Oliver, you may step down, thank you."

Judge Cole made the remark, "I will adjourn this court case until tomorrow morning, Wednesday, at 9"00 am. At the present time, all witnesses have come forward and testified under oath that Jane Linton, 74, is the serial killer of the above mentioned victims.

The Next Morning…

Marcus and Sue entered the District Court Room at 9:00 AM in the morning, as the court was called to order and our first witness for today is Sue Benson. Sue took her place on the witness stand ready for a variety of questions. Judge Cole said, "Sue, do you swear to tell the truth, the whole truth and nothing but the truth, so help you, God?" Sue replied, "I do." Judge Cole said, "Sue, we have everything on the records about your mother's past mental illness. Can you re-explain the part about your mother discontinuing her medication for the record again?" Sue said, "Mother took her medication for years until she gradually started forgetting off and on. Eventually she got to the point where she wasn't taking her medicine at all anymore and the killings started again. And they didn't stop until I caught my mother in the elevator when she tried to rob me and then threatened to kill me. Another couple, Neil and Pauline Strape, were in the elevator with us. She didn't say anything to them."

Judge Cole said, "Very well, Sue. You may step down. Thank you." Court will be in recess until 1:00 PM.

Court resumed at 1:00 PM with people filing in to take their place for the remainder of the case. Judge Cole announced, "The final witness will be Jane Linton, the accused. Jane stepped up to the witness stand to take her oath. Attorney Slater said, "Jane, will you swear to tell the truth, the whole truth and nothing but the truth, so help you, God?" Jane said, "I do." Immediately, Judge Cole asked Jane how old she is and she said 74. Judge Cole asked her, "Jane, are you innocent or guilty of these twelve killings at the Rockwood Apartment Complex from 1995 to 2003?" Jane said, "I'm innocent, your honor, of all these accusations against me. I can explain where I was at the time of all the murders and I have an alibi for everyone."

Judge Cole continued, "Jane, can you tell us where you were on some of these occasions?" Jane said, "Several times I was taking a walk or downtown shopping, and I definitely didn't have anything to do with the gassing nor cutting the elevator cable. How on earth could anyone get gas in an elevator, let alone, cut a cable? I wouldn't even know how to do something like that."

Judge Cole asked her, "Jane, may I ask you this question? Why did you fail to continue taking your medication after you got out of the mental institution?" Jane said, "I failed to take my medication because it was very expensive, it made me nauseated and dizzy sometimes and I was so busy lots of times that I actually forgot to take it."

As Judge Cole said, "So you really think that you're innocent of all twelve murders?" Jane said, "Most definitely."

Judge Cole said, "This court case will convene until tomorrow morning at 9:00 AM.

Next Morning...

Marcus and Sue were seated once again in the front row, two seats behind Jane for moral support. In all actuality, Jane kept her eyes focused on Judge Cole, looking neither left nor right. A few more witnesses were brought forward to testify, which made Jane look even more guilty. She didn't seem to mind though. She just maintained her innocence.

Judge Cole dismissed court early and said this court case would resume one week from today on June 18, 2003 at 9:00 AM, in District Court. Marcus and Sue talked to Jane for a few minutes, telling her they would be back for the final trial. Jane had a wistful, teary look on her face indicating her frame of mind and what kind of a life she had to look forward to. Jane gave Marcus and Sue a hug and two prison guards handcuffed Jane and took her back to her cell.

Marcus and Sue bid Adam and his family farewell, thanking them for their hospitality. Marcus asked them, "Could we stay with you again when we come back next week for the trial again?" And they said, "That would be fine." Marcus and Sue left for Rockwood, Illinois immediately because they had a long drive ahead of them. They drove all night, reaching Rockwood, Illinois the next day towards evening. They stopped for meal breaks only.

Different residents at the apartment complex asked them about Jane's trial, and Sue and Marcus explained to them what had taken place during the court case. Next week they will be going back again for the remainder of the trial and following that will be the sentencing.

Marcus resumes his job as janitor at the Rockwood College plus his evening job several nights a week at the Rockwood Police Department working on unsolved cases. Sue continues to work at the Murphy Finance Company in downtown Rockwood. Sue continues to walk to work and back because she doesn't know how to drive and doesn't own a car. Sometimes if there is too much walking involved, she takes the city bus transportation. Her mother, Jane didn't know how to drive and never owned a car either. Her husband Bob Linton drove a car, up until his heath deteriorated.

In Spite of what Sue's mother, Jane, is imprisoned for, Sue still misses Jane. After all, it doesn't dispel the fact she is still Sue's mother. In the evenings when Sue came home form work, she always had someone to talk to. Not anymore! Jane ruined everything, when she went on a killing spree, murdering twelve innocent victims, who were still leading fruitful, productive lives. When this trial is completely over, but never forgotten, Jane, for a woman, will always be known as "The Notorious Serial Killer from Rockwood, Illinois."

Incoming calls are permissible only on Sundays at the St. Louis prison, between 1:00-9:00 PM. Sue called Jane yesterday to visit with her, but Jane was saddened and in a bad frame of mind, and weeping at length. Sue was wasting her time and money trying to establish grounds for a conversation with her mother.

Sue tried calling her mother again today and the prison guard said she was very despondent and wouldn't speak when addressed. She also complained about not feeling well the past several days. The prison doctor diagnosed her as being very depressed, anxious and suicidal. He prescribed some anti-depressant medication for her, which she is taking.

Jane is worried about the outcome of her trial next week. When she was experiencing the suicidal tendencies why didn't she see a doctor for an evaluation and medication? What kind of an ulterior motive and distorted way of thinking would drive this woman to the heights of a notorious killing spree? Read a little farther!

# Chapter 24
## Admission of Guilt

June 17, Marcus and Sue were on their way to St. Louis, Missouri for the trial the next day of Sue's mother, Jane Linton, accused of killing twelve people at the Rockwood Apartment Complex in Rockwood, Illinois between 1995 and 2003. This trial will start tomorrow at 10:00 AM in the District Court of St. Louis, Missouri.

Sue and Marcus drove all night and stopped in to see Adam and his family, before going to District Court, across the street from some federal buildings in downtown St. Louis. When Sue and Marcus entered District Court to take their place among everybody else, about 9:45 AM, they were shocked by what they saw. Jane looked like she had aged tremendously in this past week, her hair almost snow white, shaggy and about ten pounds lighter, and her sagging face showed even more wrinkles than when they had seen her previously. Jane didn't see Marcus and Sue as court was about to begin. Jane had been talking to her attorney Mr. Slater and every once in awhile a slight smile would creep up on her pinched up little face.

Basically, the only person that will be brought to the witness stand will be Jane Linton, the accused. Judge Cole announced, "Will Jane Linton step to the witness stand, please?" He said, "Jane, will you swear to tell the truth, the whole truth and nothing but the truth, so help you,

God?" Jane said, "I do." She sat back down at the witness stand, ready to answer many repetitive questions in any way, shape or form.

Mr. Snell, the attorney for the victim's side approached Jane and said, "Jane, my first question today is, will you be giving an admission of guilt now, before myself, Judge Cole and the court?" Jane said, "Yes Mr. Snell, those are my intentions." Mr. Snell said, "Very well, Jane, proceed with your story. What precisely transpired years ago to lead up to the events?"

Jane said, "The three people I'm guilty of killing years ago were people I didn't particularly care for and had words with either on the job or otherwise. I thought I and the world would be a better place without them, so I devised a plan to do away with them. I carried out this plan, but I also got caught in the process. I was in a mental institution for three killing in ten years. The courts didn't take the insanity plea into consideration because I discontinued my medication years ago."

Mr. Snell said, "Jane, why did you discontinue your medication?" Jane said, "Like I said a week ago, I discontinued my medication because it was very expensive, sometimes it made me nauseated and dizzy, and sometimes I simply forgot to take it." Mr. Snell continued asking questions. "If that's the case, why didn't you get a cheaper medicine, that didn't make you nauseated or dizzy and make it a point to remember to take it?" Jane said, "That's right, Mr. Snell, that's what I should've done, but failed to do. Now I'm going to be suffering for it. We live and learn."

Attorney Slater also questioned her, "Jane, this is a very unusual case and we still have some unanswered questions that we'd like to clarify. How did you get a 6 foot Arizona rattlesnake into the elevator?" Jane said, "I pulled him in a box into the elevator when no one was looking." Again Attorney Slater asked her, "Jane, How did you get the pit bull into the elevator?" Jane answered, "I just brought him out in the open, into the building, while nobody was around." Attorney Slater said, "Okay, tell me this Jane, how did you get the gas to seep from underneath the floor into the elevator?" Jane said, "I went to the Rockwood Library and looked around and saw some "How to books" that described how some older elevators like the Rockwood Apartment Complex elevators have a small trap door on the side which can be opened to be able to

## BLOOD SUCKING SERIES NO. 1: THE FINAL FLOOR

work on the elevator. I opened the elevator trap door late one night when everybody was in bed, looked in and saw a little container that said, "For Gas Only," the next day around supper time I poured gas into the container and got on the elevator to see what would happen. I pushed the button for the next floor and the elevator started moving and I could smell the odor of gas seeping into the elevator from the vent inside. I hurriedly got off on the next floor." Attorney Slater said, "Okay Jane, how about explaining the cut cable, where five tenants were killed when the elevator crashed to the basement floor? How did you maneuver that?" Jane said, "That worked the same way. I went into a hardware store and told them I needed a cutter that splices cable wire and they sold me one. When the five tenants were in the elevator with the door closed, I quickly opened the panel at the top of the elevator within arm's reach and spliced the cable in half, sending the elevator crashing to the basement floor. Everything is history now." Jane said.

Attorney Snell said, "Jane, maybe you can help us with this question. It sure would help the Rockwood Police Department. I believe it was twice, that the pit bull was released among others from a fenced in area. Did you release the pit bull and the other dogs?" Jane said, "Yes, I released them both times." Attorney Snell said, "Jane, why did you release the pit bulls? They still haven't come back." Jane said, "Oh, I don't know. I was taking a walk both times and happened to walk by. I unlatched the gate, because they were jumping up to the fence continuously and no one was around."

The twelve jury members are sitting in their jury boxes, listening to Jane's testimony and her behavior on certain subjects. The jury listened intently as Jane explained the gas leak in the elevator and the cut cable wire. The jury members were talking amongst themselves saying, "What kind of a person is she? She seems kind of scary, doesn't she?" Someone else said, "I wouldn't want to meet her in a dark alley. Another person said, "Don't worry, you won't. After all these trials, I personally don't think she'll be doing too well."

The jury members are going into their jury boxes and the judge back to his bench.

Judge Cole asked "Are there any more witnesses that will come forward, please step up to the witness stand now." No one came forward, so Judge Cole said, "We will adjourn now until August 7, 2004 at 9:00 AM. That will be the sentencing of Jane Linton, 74, for the murder of twelve residents of the Rockwood Apartment Complex in Rockwood, Illinois. Marcus and Sue gave Jane a hug and goodbye kiss and went on their way, because they have a long drive ahead of them. As usual, the only stops Marcus made were to eat their meals along the way. They drove all night and arrived in Rockwood, Illinois the next day, close to suppertime. Marcus went to bed right after they got back, because he had to be at work the next morning at Rockwood College at 7:00 AM. Sue went back the Murphy Finance Company where she does the secretarial work for the company.

Marcus posted a meeting for the apartment complex for tomorrow night, Monday at 7:00 PM. It would be a question and answer period for those interested in the outcome of Sue's mother, Jane Linton's trial. Everybody knew and thought well of her until all this happened. They never thought Jane would turn into the Notorious Serial Killer of Rockwood, Illinois. Never! But, you never know, do you? The next night everybody came to the meeting to be updated on the results of the trials that have taken place. Marcus announced that the final trial will be Monday, August 7, 2004 at 9:00 a.m. at the District Court in St Louis, Missouri where Sue and I will be attending. It will consist of court formalities and the final verdict read by a member of the jury and the final sentence read by the Judge. Jane will be led out of the courtroom, handcuffed, by guards to start her sentence immediately. We can't say anymore than this until the trial is completely over."

Marcus asked, "Are there anymore questions?" And Bob raised his hand. Marcus said, "Yes, Bob, did you have a question?" Bob said, "Yes, where do you and Sue stay when you go to St. Louis?" Marcus said, "My brother Adam and his family live in St. Louis, Missouri and he invited us to stay at his house because he has lots of room. We were grateful for that because it saved us a lot of money. Once in awhile we share a meal with them and other times we eat in downtown St. Louis. When we get back to Adam's house, about a mile from downtown, Sue has her own guest room upstairs and I have a room downstairs. Our accommodations and hospitality are wonderful."

Marcus asked, "Anymore questions?" Jake asked, "Are you able to talk to Jane personally, Marcus?" Marcus answered, "When we come into the courtroom Jane is sitting with her attorney and hardly ever acknowledges us because of her depressed state at this time. This last court case, she did give us a hug, kiss and a few words, but that was all. This concludes out meeting and we will be able to tell you more when we get back next week. Thank you all for coming and goodnight."

The meeting was adjourned and everybody went back to their apartments for the evening. The night was still young, but Sue was tired from her trip, so she locked the door with the intention of going to bed early, when she heard the phone ringing. She quickly picked up the receiver and answered, "Hello." The Prison Official said, "This is the St. Louis Prison where Jane Linton is confined until sentencing next Monday, August 6. Are you her daughter, Sue Benson?" Sue said, "Yes, I am." The Prison Official said, "We are calling to tell you that your mother Jane Linton, escaped from the prison about 2 hours ago. Occasionally, we have women prison guards deliver the meals to the women prisoners, when the men prison guards are busy. Somehow, Jane, your mother, got a hold of one of the women prison guards uniforms, put it on and started delivering meals to the women prisoners. She blended right in with the other women prison guards, no one knew the difference, because no one looks that close. We also found one of the offices that's usually locked, unlocked and quite a bit of money missing from the drawer. That's the last trace of her, Sue. Actually, she's pretty shrewd and we don't even know whether we'll ever find her again. Sue, your mother is the type of person that can even outsmart a prison guard." Sue said, "I'm sure of that." The prison official continued, "The police have been searching the whole prison for about two hours, ever since we got the word that she's not in the cell and considered missing from the prison. They have also checked the outside of the prison, even though its dark now and we haven't found her. There's a chance she's in regular clothes and in a taxi or hitchhiking into downtown St. Louis, especially when she has money now." Sue said, "What are we supposed to do, come back up again? We just got home." The prison official said, "Well, it's up to you, Sue. We have an APB (All Points Bulletin) out for her capture, because she's pretty good at eluding the police. Why don't you talk it over with your friend, Marcus and see what you can come up with? Here is a number in case you have to call on one pretext or another." Sue took the number and hung up. She called Marcus' apartment and told him about the telephone conversation with the prison guard and Jane's escapade, once again. Marcus said, "I don't know how to deal with this anymore and neither does Sue. What should they do? What would you do?

Marcus and Sue talked it over and they decided to wait until the next evening to see if they have captured Jane yet. The next evening, Sue called the St. Louis Prison to see if they have captured her mother? The same prison official answered and he said, "No, Sue, your mother has never been recovered. In fact, there has never even been any sighting of her. I don't know what else tell you, I'm sorry."

Sue said, "Marcus and I are thinking about coming up, since it's so close to when we would be coming again anyway. You'll see us when we get there, Okay?" The prison official said, "Okay, that's fine."

Marcus and Sue left for St. Louis again about 8:00 PM Thursday night; driving all night and reaching Adam and his family's house about 7:00 PM Friday night. Marcus had called Adam in advance and explained the situation and Adam said, "That's fine, Marcus, come on ahead. We're glad to oblige." After Sue and Marcus brought their suitcases in and unpacked them, they headed straight for the St. Louis Prison to visit with the prison officials. While they were in the office visiting the phone rang and it was from the St. Louis Police Department downtown. They said, "An older woman answering the description of Jane Linton is sitting on a park bench in downtown St. Louis eating. They are going to check it out."

One Hour Later...

They called back and said, "No, it wasn't Jane Linton. It was someone else. Sorry! Thank you." Sue was devastated, because she was in hopes that it would be her mother, Jane. Where was her mother?

Where was she during the night? Was she sleeping in some back alley on the cement? Did she buy herself some food with that money she stole? Oh no! Did she spend it all on taxi fare?"

Sue came up with another idea. Want to hear it? She asked Marcus if they could drive around in downtown St. Louis in hopes of finding her mother and Marcus said, "Yes that's a good idea. We can do that until Sunday night, because the court case starts Monday morning at 9:00 AM and we have to be there. Let's start this afternoon. Okay?"

Sue said, "Okay."

By now, it was Friday afternoon and Marcus was driving in downtown St. Louis while Sue was watching out the window for Jane. Still, there was no sign of her, yet Marcus kept on driving. About 6:00 PM they decided to stop and eat at a diner and then back to driving again looking for Jane. It started getting dark, so they gave up and drove back to Adam's house. They searched all day Saturday and still couldn't find her. Everybody got up Sunday morning and went to church services, Adam and his family went on home, and Sue and Marcus continued looking for Jane. At dinner time Sue and Marcus stopped at a restaurant for lunch. While they were in there they happened to show a table waiter a picture of Jane and she immediately recognized her. She said, "Yes, I know her, that's Faye. She's been in here several times. If you wait, she'll probably be in here for lunch." So Sue and Marcus took their sodas and sat in the last booth in the restaurant. They waited…and waited…and waited some more and finally Jane came walking through the door, oblivious of everything around her. She sat in a booth on the opposite side of Sue and Marcus, looking despondent and sick. Marcus and Sue approached her and she barely lifted her face, nor opened her eyes to look at them, because of the shame and fear that clouded them. Sue said, "Mother, it's us. Were so glad we found you, because we've been looking for you since Friday. We were so worried about you and still are."

"Mother, you're going to have to come with Marcus and myself to the St. Louis Prison." Sue put her arm around her mother and Jane slapped them backwards. Marcus said, "Jane, lets not be doing things like that," and Jane said, "Shut up, you ugly creep! Don't tell me what to do, and stay away from my daughter. I never did like you!" Sue asked her, "Mother, are you going to order something to eat?" And Jane screamed out loud for everybody to hear, "No, I'm not and leave me alone." When Marcus heard this he went to the front counter and told the cashier, "Would you please call somebody from the St. Louis Police Department to come here to the restaurant and take my friends mother along, because they are looking for her. About twenty minutes later the St. Louis Police Department arrived, handcuffed Jane and took her in a police car to the St. Louis prison, with Sue and Marcus following. When they reached the prison they put her under twenty four hour surveillance with cameras and a prison guard posted at her cell continually until the sentencing Monday morning. By this time Jane is spitting saliva on Marcus, Sue, the prison guards, everyone she comes in contact with. She has a fiery look in her eyes like that of a wild caged animal. Has she gone completely mad? Read on!

Marcus and Sue left the prison guards to handle her and they went to Adam's house. They related the whole story and Adam and his wife shook their heads saying, "Marcus and Sue, we truly feel sorry that you had to be exposed to this terrible situation with your mother, Sue. I hope and pray that you will get through the sentencing all right." Marcus and Sue said, "Thank you," and went to their separate bedrooms.

The court case and sentencing is Tuesday, August 8, 2004. In the meantime, Marcus and Sue make an attempt to see Jane Monday, not knowing whether they can visit her at such a late date, one day before her sentencing. The prison guards said, "That's fine; time limit is 30 minute cell time visiting, I'll take you down to her cell. He took them to Jane's cell and unlocked the prison bars, which allowed them in, saying, "Jane, you have company. Your daughter, Sue, and her friend Marcus."

As soon as Jane heard this she screamed, "Get out of here! I never want to see you two again! Sue, your no daughter of mine anymore and you, Marcus, are even less than that! You brought me to this crazy place! It reminds me of an insane asylum I was confined to years ago, which I didn't deserve." Jane's eyes were piercing with fiery rage as she said, "I know tomorrow is my sentencing, the day I am dreading.

## BLOOD SUCKING SERIES NO. 1: THE FINAL FLOOR

You will never see me alive again. Goodbye!" Sue started crying and a prison guard let them through the bars, with Marcus trying to console her. They got in Marcus' car and headed for Adam's house, not knowing what to do. Sue was still crying when they were in Adam's house and no amount of consoling did any good. Sue went to her bedroom to rest while Marcus sat on the front porch talking to Adam. Marcus explained everything that transpired while they were in the prison cell, the screaming, the bitter things she said and her image of a deranged woman, a wild animal. Adam and his wife were beside themselves with a range of emotions, sympathy, anger, sadness, disgust, and powerless.

Marcus was emotionally tired of the verbal abuse he had to sustain from Jane's bitter outbursts of hatred toward him. Why did she act like that? Marcus had never done anything to Jane to offend her. Actually, he had never even spoken to her that much over the years. Was it because of his deputy job at the police department? Maybe. Or maybe because of his friendship with Sue? Was Jane jealous? Who knows? Read farther!

It had been a hot day, but it was beginning to cool off, with dark, stormy clouds moving in over the St. Louis area and a wind to follow. A soft, slow rain started clouding the horizon and pellets of hail that came later. Marcus and Sue were sitting on Adam's front porch trying to sort out their thoughts in regards to Jane's actions the day before. Whenever Marcus brings the subject up Sue starts to weep, so he changes the subject. By tomorrow night at this time, they would be on their way home.

Marcus said, "Sue lets watch television for a change. Adam and his family always watch the 10:00PM news." So they went inside just as the 10:00 PM news started. It started with the out of state and overseas news and then the local news. A few, local, issues were addressed and then the sentencing of Jane Linton was mentioned because it will be covered by the television station. The actual sentencing will be on the news tomorrow night of "The Notorious Serial Killer of Rockwood, Illinois."

# Chapter 25
# Sentencing

Marcus and sue left for District Court around 8:15 AM, in a blinding rainstorm, even though the sentencing doesn't start until 9:00 AM. If they were too early they would just have to sit and wait. They took their seats towards the front, as Jane was led into the courtroom, not looking their way. She wore a blue blouse and navy blue skirt, her hair trimmed and neatly combed, but her countenance was void of all emotions. Jane was upset and had a blank, strange stare, because her insanity plea wasn't considered at all.

The courtroom was full and the twelve jury team was in attendance in their jury boxes.

Judge Cole told Jane to arise and face the jury. A member of the jury designated to read the verdict, stood up and read the verdict, "We find the accused, Jane Linton, guilty of first degree murder in the deaths of twelve victims from Rockwood, Illinois After the verdict was read, Judge Cole said, "The accused is sentenced to life in prison, with no chance for parole. Her sentence starts immediately." Sue and Marcus looked at Jane for a reaction, but there wasn't any. Just that same, blank, motionless stare, not turning her head left or right.

Judge Cole said, "This case is closed." Two prison guards led Jane out of the courtroom and into another chamber, while everybody got up and left. Marcus said as they left, "I knew exactly what the verdict would be and I knew the sentencing also." Sue said, "So did I. It was easy to figure out." Marcus said, "Sue, did you notice your mother had no emotions on her face or in her actions. Didn't you think that quite unusual?" Sue said, "No, not really, Marcus. My mother is guilty of everything she did and then some. She deserved life in prison without parole, but that doesn't change the fact that she's still my mother." Marcus said, "I understand, Sue."

Sue was very quiet and reserved as they were driving back to Rockwood, Illinois. She was deep in thought as to what the future would bring. If she made an attempt to visit her mother, would she be welcome or would her mother scream at her and chase her out of the prison cell? What do you think? Read on!

They reached Rockwood the next day around suppertime, because they drove all night again, only stopping for meals. Marcus went to his apartment and to bed immediately because he had to be up at 6:00 AM the next morning for work. Sue went to her apartment, watched television for awhile and went to bed.

The next day Marcus posted a sign on the bulletin board for a meeting the next night, when he doesn't have to work as a deputy at the police department. It was a question and answer meeting about the sentencing and the verdict.

Everybody showed up for the meeting, anxious to hear how the sentencing part of the case turned out. Marcus explained to the residents that Sue and him had just gotten home the night before and he would answer all questions that were asked of him if the residents raised their hands. Mike raised his hand and Marcus said, "Yes, Mike. What is the question?" Mike said, "What was the actual verdict and sentencing?" Marcus said, "The actual verdict for Jane was life in prison, with no parole. The prison sentence started immediately. That's what we were told."

Phil raised his hand and asked, "What was Jane's reaction to this sentence?" Marcus said, "Nothing, she just had a blank, strange stare about her. She barely moved her head all the time she was setting there." Harold raised his hand and made the remark, "I'm very glad that she's gone, because we don't have to be afraid to ride the elevator anymore. I'm also glad she's not coming back anymore."

Albert raised his hand to make a remark. "I'm glad she's gone also, because I always felt uncomfortable around her. She wasn't that friendly to me. In fact, she hardly ever spoke to me."

Anna raised her hand to talk, saying, "She wasn't that friendly with anybody. I don't think anybody really liked her that much. We just tolerated her for Sue's sake."

Irene also raised her hand, remarking, "I didn't like to play cards with her because she would never talk to you and would always seem so snobbish. One day I remember I asked her something and she didn't even answer me and looked the other way. I had enough of her then."

"Margaret, did you have a question for us," said Marcus. Margaret, "As a matter of fact I do. I've never liked Jane since the first day I laid eyes on her. She was a little bit too quiet and a little bit on the creepy side. She made me feel nervous." Like Albert said, "She made you feel uncomfortable!"

Jacob, "My wife, Agnes, and I didn't care for Jane Linton at all anymore. When she spoke to you she was always bragging or bossing somebody. My wife and I don't like those characteristics in people, because we're not that way."

Charles made a remark, "I'm glad Sue isn't down here this evening to hear all these negative remarks being made about her mother, but there true. If she was down here I know that nobody would be saying these things."

Marcus said, "Well, at least we have everybody's input even if it isn't good, it's still how the tenants feel. We can't keep losing tenants, because there are only twenty nine of us left. I guess we all have to stick together like glue. If more tenants move out, they'll probably close the apartment complex. I hope not." Marcus said, "I don't want to move again. I just moved in here a couple of months ago. Is there anybody thinking about moving out of here?" Nobody raised their hands. Marcus said, "Good."

"Well, I guess we'll adjourn the meeting for tonight and I want to thank you all for coming. Goodnight." Everybody left the recreation parlor for their apartments, including Marcus. He hadn't eaten supper yet, so he sat in front of the 10:00 PM news eating a ham sandwich, potato chips and Pepsi, and then he went to bed.

Pinochle Night…

Marcus and the pinochle group still play cards on Tuesday nights in the recreation parlor from 7:00 PM till 10:00 PM. Marcus is already in the recreation parlor getting everything ready, while Anna donates several dozen chocolate chip cookies and Marcus makes the iced tea. Sue isn't coming down to the pinochle game this evening because she has a bad case of depression, her job performance is lacking at the Murphy Finance Company, she goes to sleep right after supper, and she's not happy, but very sad and withdrawn. She has the typical symptoms of depression.

Marcus suggested some anti-depressants to help her through this difficult time, but Sue said "I can't afford the medication." Marcus said, "I'll help you pay for your medicine," but Sue said, "No, I'd rather you didn't."

Periodically Marcus checks in on Sue to see how she's doing, but she's not getting any better. Marcus tries to pull Sue out of her shell, but it isn't working. Sue is not responding the way she should be. Marcus also confided in Pastor Hale from the Rockwood Community Church for prayers mentioned for Sue and Jane at church services tomorrow night. Pastor Hale was in agreement with the suggestion and put it at the top of the agenda for tomorrow night's service at 7:00 PM.

The services at Rockwood Community church were well attended by the apartment complex and otherwise. A special prayer service was conducted by Pastor Hale for Sue, Jane and several others to be continued next week. After services everybody went to LaBamba's Restaurant for coffee and conversation. They pushed two rectangular tables together and Marcus conducted a short informal discussion with the apartment complex tenants. Marcus said, "At this time I don't know what to do about Sue. She is very depressed, doesn't come out of her room, sleeps all the time except when she works at the Murphy

Finance Company, and I've heard her job performance leaves a lot to be desired. She's not getting any better at all. In fact she's getting worse. Does anybody have any suggestions?" Mike remarked, "Maybe, we'll just have to continue talking to her about going to the doctor. I have another suggestion. Maybe Sue can just call her doctor instead of going in and explain the situation and he can give her some free anti-depressant samples to see how they work for her. If they work maybe she can find some company that she will qualify income wise and they will send her medication free. That's what I do for the past several years now and it's been working beautifully."

Marcus said, "Mike has a good idea there. I'm going to mention this to Sue and see what she says. Does anybody have anymore suggestions in regards to Sue's problem? This discussion is over till the next time. Goodnight."

Marcus and the rest of the group went back to the apartment complex. He checked in on Sue and found her the same way. Practically no response, no medication, no interaction with the outside world and barely any food. He tried to talk to her, but she won't listen to anybody, not even Marcus. Sue is very upset because of the murders her mother committed and now is in prison for the rest of her life with no chance for parole. Plus, her mother, Jane, won't even speak to her anymore, not in person or by phone, so Sue doesn't even know whether it's worth making a trip to the St. Louis Prison or not. What should Sue do? What would you do? Let's see what happens, Okay?

A Birthday Party…

The next night is Anna Jakowski's eighty fifth birthday party and all the apartment complex tenants will be attending at 7:00 PM in the recreation parlor. The apartment complex furnished the birthday cake, ice cream, drinks, napkins, silverware and other small incidentals.

Everybody was there except Sue and she wouldn't be coming. The all sang "Happy Birthday" to Anna and did partake of the cake and ice cream. Anna requested "no gifts," but her friends and family still showered her with a variety of gifts she could use, plus money. A nice time was had by all, as they went back to their apartments.

The next morning Marcus started his janitorial work at the college at 7:00 AM like always, when all of a sudden he received a call from the Rockwood Police, calling from the hospital. What happened in as follows:

Marcus went to work and forgot to check in on Sue. Murphy Finance Company reported to the police department saying, "Sue didn't show up for work, so we are asking the police if they would check up on Sue if she's all right? The police went to the apartment complex, took the elevator to the third floor, but there was no response when they called her name. Officer Leeds kicked the door open to find Sue lying on the floor unconscious. She was bleeding profusely from slashing her wrists in a desperate attempt to take her own life. Blood was seeping onto her clothes, the carpet and anywhere it could leak onto. She could've been lying there for about two hours. No one knows for sure. The police called the paramedics to transport her to the hospital, since she was losing blood rather fast.

The ambulance came within a few minutes and took her to the Rockwood Hospital for blood transfusions and whatever other medical care she might need. On Marcus's lunch break he went to the hospital emergency room to see how Sue was doing and the nurse said, "Oh, she's back in her own room, in room 342." Marcus said, "Thank you," and continued down the hall to room 342. He went in and said, "Hello Sue." She didn't flinch either way. She smiled a little and stared straight ahead, not speaking. Marcus asked her a few question, but there was no response. He noticed that her wrists were bandaged and kind of swollen. He sat for a few minutes and then left for lack of conversation. He would come back later tonight.

Around suppertime, Marcus went back to the hospital for a quick lunch in the hospital cafeteria, and on to Sue's room. He said, "Hello Sue, how are you?" Still no answer. She did not acknowledge him, smile, or speak, nothing. She still had that weird, blank, stare and her eyes were fixed, with no normal blinking. When Marcus witnessed this strange facial expression he got up and left, because he knew definitely that something was terribly wrong.

He talked to Sue's doctor in the hallway and he said that Sue lost a considerable amount of blood after the suicide attempt, which caused her depression to get even worse. Now, they are going to have to give her shock treatments on her head to snap her back to reality and help her forget what her problem is. She also should have taken care of her depression sooner. She let it go way too long to the point where it was dangerous. Dr. Crane said, "Sue will probably be better in a couple of days. If there is a change for the worse we'll call you." Marcus said, "Thank you," and left. When he goes back to the apartment complex, he posted an update on Sue's condition saying "Sue needs prayers and God's help through this sad period in her life. Please help her. If anybody wants to visit her she is in room 342 at the Rockwood Hospital."

Instead of going to the hospital to visit Sue, Marcus just called the hospital to see how she was doing and they said, "Sorry, no change." He would go to the hospital to check Sue out again.

He went back to the hospital the next day to see if her condition had changed and it had not. Dr. Cane said, "We might have to call in a specialist from Millen Medical Center in New York City, New York, because she isn't improving." Things look pretty bad for Sue, don't they? Will she continue to live or will something fatal happen to her? Keep reading!

The Next Day...

Marcus went back to the hospital to check on Sue and Dr. Crane met with Marcus in the hallway and said, "A specialist, Dr. Simon, is flying in from Millen Medical Center in New York City arriving in Chicago, Illinois and someone will be there from the hospital to pick him up. Dr. Simon has had a lot of experience with these kinds of cases in New York City and said he's sure he'll be able to help Sue and not to worry.

Marcus had to work in the evenings at his deputy job, as he hadn't called the hospital yet either. He just decided to wait and go there today after his job as janitor at the Rockwood College. He got to the hospital around 4:00 PM and went straight to Sue's room. The minute Sue laid eyes on Marcus she went hog wild screeching, "Get out of here you dirty devil. I hate you and everyone of those tenants at the apartment. It's their fault my mother's in prison for life. When I get out of here, I'm never going to talk to anybody at the apartment again!" I said, "Get out of my room! Your all nothing but a bunch of hags and bags, a bunch of stinking idiots! GO!"

Marcus was shocked the way Sue acted, just a spitting image of Jane with her language and actions, except not the killings. But then, we don't know that do we? What did Dr. Simon do to Sue? Let's find out!

Marcus approached Dr. Simon in the hall and asked him, "Dr. Simon, what happened to my friend, Sue?" She's had a complete personality change for the worse. I don't understand this. She screams at me for no reason. This has all happened since she slashed her wrists in that suicide attempt. She wasn't like this before, I can assure you! Dr. Simon, she is acting just like her mother Jane acted, when they took her to the St. Louis Prison. Except not the murders. What went wrong?"

Dr. Simon tried to explain, "Marcus, this happens sometimes to people. After they suffer a great blood loss like Sue did, sometimes the mind reverts back into an inherited trait like that of her mother, Jane. We don't know how long this will last, a month, maybe as long as she lives. In my medical profession as a doctor, I've seen it go both ways. We'll send her home with medication, but there again; we don't know how effective it will be on Sue. On some people it works well and on others not at all." Marcus said, "In other words, it's just trial and error." Dr. Simon said, "That's absolutely correct." Dr. Simon said, "Marcus, I'm sorry to have to tell you this, but that's the way it is." Marcus said, "That's okay doctor, I understand. When is she getting dismissed from the hospital?" Dr. Simon said, "Probably in a couple of days."

Sue doesn't want Marcus in her hospital room anymore, so he won't be going back. The way Sue said, "I'll be moving to a different apartment away from Marcus. How long will this behavior last? No one knows. Remember what Dr. Simon said? Well?

Sue came back to the apartment complex two days later and was assigned a different apartment on the fourth floor, away from Marcus.

She shunned Marcus and the other tenants every chance she got. She also didn't attend any social events, parties, meeting, nothing. She doesn't work at Murphy Finance Company anymore, because she is not able to work anymore. She gets a disability check from the government every month and she lives on that. Finally, the other night, Sue decided to call her mother in the St. Louis Prison to see if she would talk to her. Surprisingly, Jane talked to Sue in a soft, quiet, refined tone, just like old times and Sue answered back. They had a nice conversation with Sue saying, "Mom. I'll be up there to see you at the prison sometime by the Greyhound Bus, I promise." Jane said, "I'm looking forward to your visit, Sue!"

Sue has nothing to do with Marcus and the rest of the tenants at the Rockwood Apartment Complex. She spends her days sleeping late, taking long walks, shopping or maybe going to a movie. The other day Sue walked to the bus terminal and asked them about the price of a round trip ticket to St. Louis and back and they said $200.00 and they gave her a schedule. Sue bought a ticket and could use it for the next year. She is planning on using it at Christmas time, because she didn't want to be by herself at Christmas. So, Sue is saving her ticket to travel on December 23rd in the morning.

## Thanksgiving and Christmas

Thanksgiving came and went and now December 23rd is here. Sue is on the morning bus headed for St. Louis, Missouri. After she gets there she will stay at the St. Louis Motel, not far from the prison. She will spend Christmas Eve at the prison with her mother Jane. She put her mothers Christmas presents in her suitcase and she hoped she liked them. Her mother, Jane, knows she's coming and so do some of Jane's friends at the prison. When she arrived, she received a warm welcome from Jane, her friends and the staff. Sue spent Christmas Eve with Jane and her friends and left by bus to go back to Rockwood, Illinois December 26th. It was a long ride back, but she enjoyed it. She will be coming back again next summer. This was fun.

She arrived back in Rockwood, Illinois with a light snow falling at 11:00 PM. She took a taxi to the apartment complex and let herself in with her key. She encountered Marcus coming down the hall saying, "Hello Sue." Sue looked at Marcus, her eyes glowing like fire, "Get away from me, you and your slimy friends. Your nothing but a son of a bitch. One of these days I might kill you, Marcus, you never know." Sue gave Marcus a weird look and strange laugh that would make you shudder, kind of eerie.

Marcus walked away but from then on he never forgot those words about Sue killing him… Would she really do it? She seems like the second Jane. Maybe he should move out of the apartment complex to get away from her, because he doesn't trust Sue anymore. He's thinking strongly about moving out because of what she said.

Sue continues to visit her mother, Jane, at the St. Louis Prison for Women occasionally. Would you trust Sue?